Double the DANGER and ZERO Zucchini

ALSO BY BETSY UHRIG

Welcome to Dweeb Club

DOUBLE the DANGER and ZERO Zucchini

BETSY UHRIG

MARGARET K. McELDERRY BOOKS

NEW YORK LONDON TORONTO SYDNEY NEW DELHI

MARGARET K. McELDERRY BOOKS
An imprint of Simon & Schuster Children's Publishing Division
1230 Avenue of the Americas, New York, New York 10020

This book is a work of fiction. Any references to historical events, real people, or real places are used fictitiously. Other names, characters, places, and events are products of the author's imagination, and any resemblance to actual events or places or persons, living or dead, is entirely coincidental.

Text © 2020 by Betsy Uhrig
Cover illustration © 2020 by Linzie Hunter
Cover design by Rebecca Syracuse © 2020 by Simon & Schuster, Inc.
All rights reserved, including the right of reproduction in whole or in part in any form.
MARGARET K. McELDERRY BOOKS is a trademark of Simon & Schuster, Inc.
For information about special discounts for bulk purchases, please contact Simon & Schuster Special Sales at 1-866-506-1949 or business@simonandschuster.com.
The Simon & Schuster Speakers Bureau can bring authors to your live event. For more information or to book an event, contact the Simon & Schuster Speakers Bureau at 1-866-248-3049 or visit our website at www.simonspeakers.com.
Also available in a Margaret K. McElderry Books hardcover edition
Interior design by Rebecca Syracuse
The text for this book was set in Athelas.
Manufactured in the United States of America
0722 OFF
First Margaret K. McElderry Books paperback edition September 2021
2 4 6 8 10 9 7 5 3
The Library of Congress has cataloged the hardcover edition as follows:
Names: Uhrig, Betsy, author.
Title: Double the danger and zero zucchini / Betsy Uhrig.
Description: First edition. | New York : Margaret K. McElderry Books, an imprint of Simon & Schuster Children's Publishing Division, 2020. | Audience: Ages 8–12. | Audience: Grades 4–6. | Summary: While brainstorming ideas to improve his aunt's boring children's book, 12-year-old Alex and his friends begin to act out new scenes that will make the plot more exciting . . . and dangerous.
Identifiers: LCCN 2020009407 (print) | ISBN 9781534467651 (hardcover) | ISBN 9781534467675 (eBook)
Subjects: LCSH: Books and reading—Juvenile fiction. | Authorship—Juvenile fiction. | Aunts—Juvenile fiction. | Friendship—Juvenile fiction. | Humorous stories. | CYAC: Books and reading—Fiction. | Authorship—Fiction. | Aunts—Fiction. | Friendship—Fiction. | Humorous stories. | LCGFT: Humorous fiction.
Classification: LCC PZ7.1.U3 Do 2020 (print) | DDC 813.6 [Fic]—dc23
LC record available at https://lccn.loc.gov/2020009407
ISBN 9781534467668 (pbk)

For Dad

DOUBLE the DANGER and ZERO ZUCCHINI

1

MY NAME IS ALEX HARMON. Unless you actually know me, I'm sure you've never heard of me. Because I'm not famous in any way. And I wouldn't want to be. In fact, I'd rather dive into the back of a garbage truck with my mouth open than be famous.

Part of this is because I'm not naturally outgoing, but part of it is because I know someone who is famous and have seen a small sliver of what it's like. The mail volume alone is staggering. Did you know people still write letters on paper? Those really pile up.

The famous person I know is R. R. Knight. I bet you've heard of R. R. Knight. You can't even go to the grocery store without bumping into a cardboard display full of R. R. Knight books: *Gerald in the Warlock's Weir* and the new one, *Gerald in the Grotto of the Gargoyles.* Maybe you waited in line at midnight for *Gerald in the Grotto of the Gargoyles* (and if you did, I salute you). Even if you hardly ever read books, you've probably read at least one of the Gerald books. Which is why their author is so famous.

But let me ask you this: How old is R. R. Knight? What color hair does R. R. Knight have? Is R. R. Knight a dog person or a cat person?

You might think R. R. Knight looks like your cool uncle: tall, with a little beard. Maybe a hat of some kind. But that's just a picture you have in your head. The kid sitting next to you on the bus right now would probably disagree. She might say that R. R. Knight looks like her fun grandmother: short, with gray hair and those glasses with no frames that you can still tell are glasses.

And let me ask you this: What does R. R. stand for? You don't know, do you? And your teachers don't know. Even the librarian at the main branch doesn't know.

Well, you say, no one knows what R. L. or J. R. R. stand for either. To which I can reply, after a few minutes of googling: Robert Lawrence and John Ronald Reuel (and why don't we see kids named Reuel anymore?).

Now try it for R. R. Anything? Anything at all? Nope. Nothing. No names, no photos—with or without hats or glasses—no birthdate, no hometown, no family. Only books.

Curious? I would be too. Who is this "famously reclusive author" (says Wikipedia) loved by even the most reluctant readers?

That's what I'm here to tell you. It's a long story, though not nearly as long as *Gerald in the Grotto of the Gargoyles*—that thing should come with a handle. I'm here to give you the background that people have been asking for about the mysterious R. R. Knight. But don't worry—this isn't in any way a biography. That would be impossible. Because R. R. Knight doesn't exist.

2

"**GERALD RAN UP THE FRONT STEPS** to his grandfather's house."

That's how it begins, right? Those are the opening words of *Gerald in the Warlock's Weir,* Book 1 in the series. You first read them after it was published, of course. I, on the other hand, read them about a year earlier, when I was twelve. Before, technically, the book was even written.

It was a Saturday afternoon in the middle of that blank, gray stretch of winter that seems to go on forever. I was up in my room, minding my own business. My mother and her sister, my aunt Caroline, were in the kitchen. I could hear them talking, but I certainly wasn't paying any attention to what they were talking about. Until I heard a familiar phrase waft up from below like a bad smell. And that phrase was "reluctant reader."

No one ever said it when they thought I would hear, but I knew it referred to me. I heard it in second grade, as I waited outside my classroom while my parents talked to my teacher. I heard it again in fourth grade, when my teacher was speaking to the school librarian during our class's library time. I heard it from my father, talking to the children's book expert at our local bookstore.

And here it was again, this time from my mother.

Now that I knew they were talking about me, I tuned in.

"Then he'd be perfect," said Caroline. "He's exactly what I need. Just let me ask him, okay? If he says no, I promise I won't bring it up again."

If this sounds like my mother and my aunt were plotting to use me as a guinea pig in an unpleasant experiment, it's because that's exactly what they were doing.

"Alex," my mom called, "can you come down here? Aunt Caroline wants to ask you for a favor."

If this were fiction and not my actual life, I would have taken the opportunity to climb out my bedroom window and run away for a wild adventure. But it was a long drop from my window. And besides, Aunt Caroline wasn't a mad scientist. She worked in an office. She wasn't going to hook me up to a machine and switch my personality with an actual guinea pig's.

As I walked slowly down the stairs, I decided that Aunt Caroline wanted to use me as a test for her childproofing. Caroline and her wife, my aunt Lulu, were having a baby in a few months. But they were carrying on like they were expecting a visit from really judgmental royalty. The paint in the baby's room had to be the perfect shade of "early-twilight blue." The carpet had been changed out twice for not being "plush" enough. And they were childproofing as if they expected their infant to leap out of their arms and start guzzling the poisons under the kitchen sink within seconds of its arrival in their home.

Some of these excessive precautions might have had to do

with my little brother, Alvin. There was some history there.

I arrived in the kitchen, resigned to crawling around Caroline and Lulu's house trying to poison, strangle, and electrocute myself. But that wasn't the favor at all. It wasn't nearly as fun.

Caroline wanted me to read a book.

3

AUNT CAROLINE HAD WRITTEN A BOOK for kids my age and needed a "test reader," she said.

The stack of paper on the kitchen table was on the small side. At least she'd had the courtesy to write a short book. But still. Not only was it a book—it was a book that someone I knew had written. How could that be any good?

"Why don't you have Alvin read it?" I asked. "He'll read anything."

Alvin was eight and the opposite of a reluctant reader. He was what parents and teachers and librarians called a "voracious reader." Which sounded much cooler than it is. It sounded as if Alvin swam around like a shark, pulling struggling books down into the depths and devouring them whole. In reality, he sat on his bed for hours at a time, almost motionless, reading and popping the occasional Cheeto into his mouth.

"That's the point," said Caroline. "We thought you'd be better, since you're . . . harder to please."

"You mean a reluctant reader."

"Not at all!" said Caroline.

"Because I'm not. I just have a bunch of other stuff I'd rather be doing."

"Which is the definition of 'reluctant,'" my mother said.

It isn't. But I didn't know that at the time.

The fact was, I preferred doing things that didn't involve so much sitting still and paying attention. Like running—anytime, anywhere. On the soccer field, down the sidewalk, in the halls at school when I could get away with it. And if I *was* going to sit still and pay attention, I preferred watching a movie or a TV show or a video online to reading. I was also a pretty good cook. So at least I was well rounded, even if I wasn't well read.

I still hadn't touched Caroline's book or even gotten too close to it.

"I was hoping to have someone who doesn't necessarily love reading try it to see if it holds their interest," said Caroline. She sighed and fiddled with the end of her ponytail. "Here's the thing. A couple of my friends have read it, and Lu read it, and they say it's great—really well written and touching and sweet."

That didn't sound like a book I'd want to read, but I was no judge—I didn't want to read most books.

"But Lu has a friend who's a literary agent," Caroline continued, twisting her hair around her finger so tight, the fingertip started to turn red. "You know—the people who sell books to publishers? And she read it as a favor to Lu. And . . ." Another sigh. "She had a different take on it."

"What did she say?" I asked.

My mother looked up from her mug of tea. Apparently, she'd been too polite to ask what the agent had said, but she was clearly curious.

"She said the writing was strong, but . . ." Caroline shifted in her chair and freed her finger from her ponytail. "But that a book for kids your age can't just be well written. She said it needs to compete with screens—'including the ones in windows,' as she put it."

Ouch, I thought.

"So it can't be boring," I said out loud.

"Right. It can't be boring. And I'm hoping you'd be willing to tell me if any of it is boring."

"Seriously? You want me to read it and point out the boring parts?" That was kind of how I read everything—in my head, at least.

"Seriously. Take a pen and circle the boring parts. I'll even pay you."

"Caroline!" said my mother. "You don't need to pay your nephew to do you a simple favor."

"Ten bucks," said Caroline to me. "Be brutal."

"You got it." I grabbed the stack of paper and headed upstairs.

THE FIRST THING I READ WAS Caroline's name and address. So far so good. Then the title: *Gerald Visits Grampa*. Which was not terribly encouraging. Because I'm sure you will agree that that title made it sound like a picture book, not a book for kids my age, which was what Caroline had said it was.

I kept going, though. Ten bucks, right? Ten very easy bucks. And there was that first sentence about Gerald arriving at his grandfather's house.

Well, mystery solved, you're thinking. R. R. Knight is the aunt of a kid named Alex Harmon—Caroline something. That's that, then. On to something else, maybe a screen of some kind.

Not so fast. My aunt Caroline is not R. R. Knight. If she were, then R. R. Knight would just be a pen name—like Dr. Seuss (Theodor Geisel) or Lewis Carroll (Charles Lutwidge Dodgson). It's more complicated than that. So I'm afraid you're going to have to keep reading.

Which is what I did. I read about Gerald's entry into his grandfather's house. It became clear over the next few sentences that Gerald was, for some reason, a frog. Gerald was a frog who

9

behaved in all ways like a human. So why was he a frog? I got a red pen out of my desk and wrote in the margin the way my teachers did on my papers: "Why a frog?"

Which felt good. For once I was the wielder of the all-questioning, all-criticizing Red Pen of Doom. I kept reading, enjoying my power.

And, well, Gerald was indeed visiting his grandfather (who was also a frog, so at least it was consistent). But I was only on page 3, and now the stack of paper was starting to look pretty thick, and there seemed to be a lot of words left to go between me and my ten dollars.

Gerald's grandfather was a grump, it turned out. But then Gerald offered to help him in the garden and . . . I'll spare you the details. Because by page 10, I had to admit that I was losing interest. I couldn't take my red pen and circle the boring parts because—I feel bad saying it even now, but it's true—*Gerald Visits Grampa* was boring. It didn't have boring parts—it was a boring whole. It didn't have any interesting parts.

My right leg jiggled the way it does when I'm getting restless. I started skimming, thinking that maybe Gerald would get sucked down a storm drain and Grampa would rescue him. Or—better—Grampa could get sucked down a storm drain and Gerald could rescue *him*. That didn't happen. And if it had, I realized, frogs swim really well anyway. I skimmed faster, in bigger chunks of pages. Then I flipped to the last page, even though the suspense wasn't exactly killing me.

In the end, in case you're curious, Gerald and Grampa won a blue ribbon for the biggest zucchini at the county fair. Which was nice for them. Not so great for the reluctant reader, though, who really needed more action to stay interested.

So now I was in a bad position. It felt as if I had a nasty book report hanging over my head. Only, the book's author and the person I was writing the report for were both my aunt.

5

I DECIDED TO GO FOR A RUN. That would give me a chance to think and also put some distance between me and Caroline and her book. I changed into my cold-weather running clothes and went downstairs.

"You can't possibly be done already," my mother said as I passed the kitchen.

"Ah, no—of course I'm not done," I said. "Just going for a run, then I'll get right back to it."

"You don't need to rush," said Caroline. "Take your time." I could see her fight with herself for a few seconds and then lose. "How are you liking it so far?" she couldn't stop herself from asking.

I had almost made it out the door. So close. *So close.* But here I was, being asked the question I was trying to literally run away from. And here's what I did (never do this, by the way): I gave my aunt a huge cheesy grin and a thumbs-up. I'm embarrassed even picturing how I must have looked.

As I was closing the door behind me, I heard Caroline say, "He's really into the whole running thing, isn't he?"

"Yup," my mom said. "Everywhere he goes. It's kind of strange, actually, but have you seen his little calf muscles? They're so—"

I took off.

I didn't have a destination in mind at first. But as I ran, I realized I was headed for Javier's house. My friend Javier lived a fifteen-minute run away, which would give me at least half an hour to decide what to tell Caroline. Plus, he had a lot of relatives, so he might have some advice on dealing with one who had written a book.

Before I could get to Javier's, though, I needed to make it past Marcello. Marcello was the neighbors' tiny rat-dog, who escaped his house every time anyone opened a door. Sure enough, he sprang out in front of me on the sidewalk, hysterically yapping the yap version of "You shall not pass." I didn't pass. As usual, I stepped over him, and he chased me until someone shook the treat jar on his front porch.

That obstacle overcome, I went on my way.

Javier lived in a big Victorian house on a street with lots of similar houses. Two doors down from him was the Old Weintraub Place, as my mother called it. It had been empty since Mrs. Weintraub moved away to live with her daughter a few years ago. It hadn't started out creepy, but it was getting there now, and I tended to run faster passing it. Today I stopped instead.

Because it occurred to me how much more interesting Caroline's book would be if Gerald's grandfather's house was slightly creepy, like this one. Maybe the porch could be creaky, like the Weintraub porch looked. Maybe there could be cobwebs like the Weintraub cobwebs. Maybe there could even be a feeling of danger as Gerald waited for his grandfather to come to the door.

I turned around and ran back the way I'd come. I didn't want this idea for some creepiness and danger to slip away before I could suggest it to Caroline. I only hoped that Javier hadn't seen me get almost to his house and then run away. He'd think I was losing my mind.

6

R u losing yr mind? THE TEXT FROM JAVIER SAID when I got home. **Why did you run away from my house?**

Long story, I wrote back. **Relative stuff.**

Say no more, Javier wrote.

He used baffling expressions like "say no more" a lot—I had no idea where they came from. If he used one often enough, I eventually started using it too. At some point we were both going to sound like characters in a PBS drama. Except no—our friend Marta would never let us get away with that. We were safe as long as she was around to ridicule us.

I changed out of my sweaty clothes, grabbed Caroline's pages, and made another note in the margin below "Why a frog?" This one said: "Some creepiness and a feeling of danger would be good." Then I headed downstairs with the book.

Caroline and my mom were still at the kitchen table. I honestly don't know how adults can sit for so long.

"I have an idea," I said.

"About the book?" asked Caroline. She pulled her ponytail in front of her and started twirling the end around her finger.

My mom flashed me a look that said, *Warning! Trouble ahead. Warning!*

It was possible, I could see now, that Caroline might not be totally happy with my having an idea about her book. But if she didn't want outside input, she shouldn't have offered me ten bucks to supply it.

"I was thinking," I said, "that you might want a feeling of danger at the beginning. To keep people's interest."

"Danger?" said Caroline. "In a children's book?"

I nodded. "To add some suspense, you know?"

"Um, sure," said Caroline. "Okay. Something to draw them in."

She let go of her hair, which I took as a good sign.

"Right. I was thinking Gerald could get to the house and it could be sort of creepy. Maybe the porch is creaky, and there are cobwebs."

"Doesn't that imply some poor housekeeping on Grampa's part?" my mom asked unhelpfully. She's kind of a stickler about cleanliness.

Caroline knew this and ignored her. "And that would make you keep reading?" she asked me.

"Yeah," I said. "Though you need to keep it going past the first page. Maybe Gerald could knock and there's no answer. So he tries the door, and it's not locked, and he goes inside. And it's kind of gloomy in there and he can't find his grampa." I was starting to enjoy this. Writing a book wasn't hard at all.

"Right!" said Caroline. "Then Grampa can come up from the

basement or something, startle him a bit. That would be fun."

"Kind of too soon, though, isn't it?" I said. "For the whole danger thing to end?"

"I like it when things work out well," said Caroline.

And who doesn't, in real life? But in books, if everything worked out well . . . we'd have nothing but *Gerald Visits Grampa*s, wouldn't we?

"Sure," I said. "But they need to work out well later. Not right there at the beginning. How about this?" I asked, and now I was just freewheeling, saying stuff as it entered my head, maybe even before. "How about Gerald can't find Grampa anywhere? Grampa is missing. And Gerald starts to sense a Presence in the house. . . ."

Caroline had taken a notebook out of her bag and was writing. I wrote in the margins of the book at the same time: "Gerald senses Presence. Grampa missing. Where is he?"

"Not 'presence,'" I said, looking over her shoulder at her notes. "It should be 'Presence,' with a capital *P*."

"What difference does it make?"

"A Presence is way creepier. Trust me."

She capitalized it. I was pleased.

"This is a lot to think about," she said. But she sounded more excited than whiny. "I'm going to have to rewrite the whole beginning."

"Not the first sentence," I said. "The first sentence is fine the way it is."

"That's a relief," said Caroline.

I was feeling pretty impressed with myself when Caroline left. She said she was going to follow my suggestions and see what I thought when she was done. She asked me to send her any other ideas I had. She tried to give me the ten dollars then and there, but my mom said I hadn't earned it yet.

The beginning of the book was looking more interesting now. But books can't just be interesting, I knew. They also have to be believable. You have to feel like you're there, inside the character's head, or at least really close by. And to make it believable, you need realistic details. "Write what you know," my teachers were always saying. And I didn't know anything about what it was like to wander around in a creepy empty house.

I did, however, know how to find out.

7

MY MOM WORKED FROM HOME AS a graphic designer, but she ran a pet-sitting business on the side. Probably because she never met an animal she didn't adore (even Marcello) and my dad was allergic to fur and had a sneeze like a cannon blast. Mom's "office" was the desk in the back hall, over which was a pegboard with keys hanging from it—the keys to the houses of the people she pet-sat for. And on that pegboard hung a key to the Old Weintraub Place, because my mom took care of Mrs. Weintraub's cats before Mrs. Weintraub and the cats moved in with her daughter.

I was back in the same sweaty running clothes from before, my day pack filled with Caroline's book and the Red Pen of Realistic Details. On the way out the door, I ever so casually grabbed the Weintraub key from the Weintraub hook and tossed that in as well. Then I ran to Javier's house.

Javier was ready for me because I'd gotten good at texting and running at the same time without breaking my face on the sidewalk. I did break my phone once, though.

"Where's Great-Aunt Rosa?" I asked when I got to his front porch.

Javier's great-aunt Rosa sat outside on the porch swing a lot, reading paperback books the size of bricks. Even when it was cold, like today, she bundled up and kept a hot drink nearby. According to Javier, she came out there to get away from the rest of the family.

He shrugged. "The senior center, most likely. She's been spending a lot of time there since Great-Aunt Marina moved in with us."

Great-Aunt Rosa almost never said anything to me, and she never, ever cracked a smile, but I sort of missed seeing her.

Javier and I sat on the porch swing, and I described my situation for him.

"You do *not* want to criticize a relative's art," said Javier. "That never ends well."

"So I'm thinking I could let myself into the Old Weintraub Place," I said. "To see what it's like. And film it so I can remember the details. Then I'll report back to Caroline, and she can add it to the book. That's helping, not criticizing, right?"

"Can't you just *imagine* what it's like in there?" Javier asked. "Isn't that what writers do? Imagine stuff and then write it down?"

"Sure, *writers* do that," I said. "But I'm not a writer, am I? And I have no imagination. You know that from creative writing last year."

He did know that—he'd been my partner. We were both grateful when we'd moved on to persuasive essays.

"All right," Javier said. "Just to clarify: by 'I' you mean 'we' in this case? *We* can let ourselves in and see what it's like? And no one but you calls it the Old Weintraub Place, by the way. It doesn't have, like, landmark status."

"Fine," I said. "And of course I mean 'we.' One of us to do the experiencing—that would be me—and the other to do the filming. That would be you. Obviously."

Javier had been making films since he got a video camera for his birthday a year ago. Sometimes he made stop-action films with Lego creatures, but mostly he filmed live-action sequences of Marta doing reckless stunts.

"Cool," said Javier. "I'll get my camera."

8

JAVIER FILMED FROM THE FRONT WALK as I ran, à la Gerald, up the steps of the Old Weintraub Place.

The porch was good and creaky, and the spiderwebs were a nice touch.

"Are you getting all this?" I asked Javier.

"All what?"

"The sensory detail. Like we were always supposed to be using in creative writing."

"I'm getting the sights and sounds," Javier said. "This camera doesn't record the other senses. If you want to lick the railing, be my guest."

I did not want to lick the railing. There was probably bird poop all over it.

I took a sniff of the air instead. I smelled the evergreens next to the steps, which was pleasant.

Then I put my hand on the front door and felt the roughness of the wood and the crackly edges of the peeling paint. Excellent. Caroline would love this stuff. I got out her book and my Red Pen of Inspiration and jotted some notes in the margin.

Then I got out the key and put it in the lock. The lock was not happy about being used at first, but it gave in eventually. I opened the door slowly and stepped into the house. Javier followed at filming distance. When he got inside, I closed the door so the neighbors wouldn't see us and think we were robbers.

The evergreen smell was gone, replaced by something more like old dust. The floorboards creaked louder in the quiet house than the porch ones had outside. The front hall was dim and, I was happy to see, kind of creepy. Perfect. To my right: the living room, the furniture covered with sheets so it looked like ghost furniture. To my left: the dining room—with the ghosts of a table and chairs. Over the table hung a chandelier-type light draped with cobwebs.

I pointed at it.

"I see it," said Javier, aiming the camera at the ceiling.

"Grampa," I called experimentally. "Are you here?"

"You're not really going to—" Javier began.

"Of course not!" I said. "This is just to know how it would sound."

"All right," said Javier. "Have at it. But you probably need to call a little louder. Grampas can be hard of hearing."

Javier had way more experience with grampas than I did. He had at least three, maybe more kicking around. I didn't have any.

I called a little louder: "Grampa?" Then I turned to Javier. "Are you getting this?"

"If you ask me that again, we are done."

"Okay, okay."

I moved down the hall toward the back of the house, past what looked like a den or library—lots of shelves, nothing on them—and then a closet (empty) and a bathroom (antique). I wrote a few more notes on Caroline's pages.

"Marta would be loving this," said Javier with a tinge of guilt in his voice.

"A little too much," I said. "But we don't need to feel bad. She's grounded, anyway."

"What was it this time?"

"Cutting bangs for herself."

"That sounds about right."

She hadn't just cut bangs for herself. She'd cut bangs and decided she didn't like the look. Then, instead of simply waiting for them to grow out, she'd cut them all the way off, leaving a strip of stubble across her forehead.

"Maybe Grampa fell in the tub," said Javier, gesturing with his chin at the bathroom. "You better get in there and check it out."

I was starting to wish I was filming this myself, alone. But I went into the bathroom and opened the brittle shower curtain. And let out a scream that Javier has told me he will never, ever delete no matter what I offer him or threaten him with.

9

YOU KNOW THOSE LOZENGE-SHAPED BUGS WITH the zillions of legs that seem too disorganized to move the bug in a specific direction but somehow work really well, and the direction it moves in is always, always at your face? The biggest of those bugs ever was living in the folds of the Weintraub shower curtain. If Grampa had fallen in the tub, he would have been eaten.

The enormous bug lunged at me—I'm not exaggerating. It lunged at my face, and of course I screamed. Of course I batted at it with the book and the Red Pen of Self-Defense and yelled, "Get it off me! Get it off me!" even though it wasn't, it turned out, on me at all.

Javier didn't flinch as it ran between his sneakers, but he probably didn't even notice it due to his laughing. When Javier was serious, he had the dignity of a statue. But when he laughed the way he was laughing now, he totally lost it. He had to set the camera down on the sink, he was laughing so hard.

"Oh, you're just great in a crisis," I said. "Thanks so much for your help there."

"When you say 'crisis,' do you mean 'little tiny centipede'?"

"It was gigantic," I said. "And for all we know, that one was a baby, and the mother is about to come after us, protecting her young."

"I think you may be confusing centipedes and grizzly bears," said Javier, picking up his camera. "There's a major difference in size there, and also level of ferociousness and maternal instinct. Also, I'm pretty sure that, in terms of habitat, grizzly bears aren't commonly found in shower curtains."

"Well, neither are dangerous bugs! It caught me by surprise, is all."

Actually, most centipedes aren't dangerous—to humans, anyway—according to Wikipedia. But in my defense, and for the record, it also says that "their size and speed can be startling." So there.

If you've read *Gerald in the Grotto of the Gargoyles*, you might have recognized the Belligerent Bug that attacks Gerald in chapter 3. It is indeed an overgrown, eerily glowing centipede. Only, that one is extremely dangerous to humans. It's also fictional. But Gerald's scream when it attacks him? That is based on fact. Javier still has the recording, and he'd be glad to show it to you.

10

I CLOSED THE DOOR TO THE bathroom once we'd gotten back into the hallway and I had finished frantically combing my fingers through my hair to make sure no bugs were clinging to it.

"You realize that a bug could simply walk under that door," said Javier. "There's plenty of head clearance there for a bug."

"It will at least slow them down," I said. "Especially if there's any kind of swarming situation. Come on, let's check out the kitchen."

"I don't know," said Javier, camera on again. "What if a gang of sarcastic ladybugs is hanging around in there?"

I chose not to respond to this, and it was during my silence that we heard the Noise. We both froze, though Javier, a true pro, kept filming.

It wasn't a small-*n* noise. It was a capital-*N* Noise. It wasn't one of those random noises that you would hear in an empty old house as you blundered around pretending to search for your missing grampa. It was a precise Noise. The kind that indicates a Presence.

And here I have to admit that up until this point, I'd been sort of hoping for some sign of a Presence, so I could tell Caroline what it was like to feel one. But now, faced with an actual Noise and a possible actual Presence making the Noise, I wasn't happy at all. There was still some adrenaline going from the centipede ambush, and it all added up to more suspense than I wanted in my real life.

While this was going on in my head, here's what was going on in Javier's:

"Raccoons in the trash, maybe? Squirrels in the attic?"

The fact that he hadn't said "Enormous mother centipede out for revenge?" meant that he was taking the Noise seriously. Which on the one hand I appreciated. And on the other I didn't, because when Javier took something seriously, that meant it was truly serious.

"Maybe," I said. "But if they're active during the day, doesn't that mean they're rabid?"

"Raccoons, yes," he said. "Squirrels, no."

I had no idea how he knew these things. We were in the same class at the same school—we should have had the same information. Yes, he'd already had the growth spurt that I was still waiting for, but a bigger head didn't mean a smarter brain. Or did it? I'd have to ask him later.

"Maybe you should go first," I said, instead of, *Maybe we should run out the front door and keep running*, which was definitely my first impulse. "Change up the angle and film me from the front walking toward the kitchen."

Javier saw right through that obvious ploy.

"Get going," he said.

"I wish I had a stick or something," I said. The pen and the pages of Caroline's book weren't much good as weapons, I already knew.

"So do I," Javier muttered in a tone that made it very clear who he would have been poking if he'd had a stick handy.

I walked slowly toward the kitchen, worried about the Noise. Worried about a Presence. Worried about not having a stick. And, most of all, worried about screaming again.

11

THE KITCHEN WAS A RELIEF. AT first, anyway. It was less dim than the rest of the house because there were no shades or curtains over the windows. The table and chairs weren't covered with sheets. The floor and counters were clean, and the appliances were shiny. Even my mom wouldn't have been able to criticize. Which, as I said, came as a relief—until Javier had to go and mention, "This place doesn't look abandoned at all. Check it out—there are dishes in the drying rack."

There were. And they weren't coated with dust. They looked freshly washed.

"Maybe someone comes in to clean once in a while?" I suggested.

"They're not doing a good job in the bathroom," said Javier. "And they missed something. Look." He pointed with the camera at the table. A mug sat on it, half filled with brown liquid.

"Ick," I said. "Is that ancient sludge in there?"

"Looks like fresh coffee," said Javier. "Go on," he said. "You're the one who's so interested in sensory details. Smell it."

I did not want to put my nose into a mug half filled with

suspicious brown liquid. Javier already had footage of me screaming and flailing around. Me puking wasn't going to happen.

"Uh-uh," I said.

He rolled his eyes. "I can smell it from here. It's coffee."

I went over to the table and studied the mug. It did look like coffee. I edged closer. Now I could smell it. Javier was right. It was coffee.

How was that possible? Was coffee a substance like Twinkies that stayed fresh no matter how long you left it out? Was there some postapocalyptic world in which humans would be long gone but their Twinkies and their coffee remained for the radioactive cockroaches to feast upon?

I put the book on the table and picked up the mug, I guess thinking I would dump the coffee out in the sink. Leave the place a little neater than I'd found it, like a good trespasser should. But as soon as I picked it up, I realized that the mug was warm.

If you've ever picked up something that you were expecting to be cool and it was warm instead, you will understand what happened next.

I let out what I'm going to call a yelp and what Javier insisted was another scream, and dropped the mug.

12

THE MUG WAS TOUGH. IT DIDN'T shatter or even chip when it hit the floor. It bounced, sending the warmish coffee splattering.

Javier wasn't laughing this time. He was looking at me like it was my sanity pooling on the linoleum and he was wondering how he was going to subdue me long enough to get me the help I needed.

"It was *warm*," I said. "The coffee was warm. How is that possible?"

I already knew what my theory was. "This place must be haunted," I said as I mopped up the coffee spill with a paper towel from the roll by the sink. "A ghost's ectoplasm must have come into contact with the liquid and heated it up."

"Haunted by who?" said Javier. "Mrs. Weintraub isn't dead."

"That we know of," I said. "And what about Mr. Weintraub? There must have been a Mr. Weintraub at some point, but we never hear about him, do we?"

"It's also possible," said Javier from behind his camera, "that a cleaning person was here, doing some cleaning and having a nice cup of coffee, and we scared them."

I was relieved to be moving away from the haunting theory.

Unfortunately, the cleaning-person theory wasn't working for me.

"Why would a cleaning person be scared by two kids?" I said. "Shouldn't they have come out of the kitchen and said, 'Hey, you kids. You're trespassing. Scram.'"

"People don't say *scram* in this century," said Javier. "But I see your point. So maybe it was another trespasser."

"A trespasser who drinks coffee and likes to keep things neat and clean?"

"You're a trespasser and you're cleaning right now."

I was. I was on my knees, drying the floor with a fresh wad of paper towels. I had already rinsed the mug and put it in the drying rack with the other dishes.

"Here's the problem, though," said Javier after a moment of filming me from behind as I worked.

"What problem?" I said, having lost the thread of the conversation.

"What if, when we scared the neat, coffee-drinking trespasser, we didn't scare them all the way out of the house? What if we only scared them into, like, a closet?" He pointed toward the pair of closed doors next to the fridge. One was probably the door to the basement, the other maybe a pantry or a broom closet. All good hiding places.

And now the memory of the Noise came back to us. Along with the feeling that a Presence could be lurking very nearby.

"We should get out of here," I said.

"Agreed," said Javier.

13

SO WE LEFT THE OLD WEINTRAUB PLACE in a hurry. And we didn't stop hurrying until we were on Javier's porch again. We reviewed the recording, from my running up the front steps, all carefree and optimistic, to the overlong footage of my butt as I dried the kitchen floor.

"Will this do?" said Javier.

"I think it will," I said. "Once you delete that last section."

"As if," my friend said quietly.

It wasn't until I was home that I remembered Caroline's book. Which was still sitting on the kitchen table in the Old Weintraub Place. All my ideas about making the story interesting. All my sensory details.

Crud. I was going to have to go back there and get it. But not today. First I would give the trespasser / cleaning person / ghost of Mr. Weintraub time to clear out. And even I was tired of running back and forth to Javier's neighborhood.

I took a shower, after carefully checking the shower curtain, of course. Then I killed the time until dinner trying to get past Chin Level on my current favorite game, Pimple Patrol.

*

Javier and I went back to the Old Weintraub Place on Sunday afternoon. He wasn't thrilled by the idea, but he went anyway, which was the kind of thing that made him a good friend.

I used the key to open the front door again, and without pausing for any sensory details or bug attacks, we hurried into the kitchen, where we found the book on the table. There was no coffee this time—everything was exactly as we'd left it.

Or so we thought until we got back to Javier's house.

First of all, and hard to miss: There was a brown ring on the first page of the book. The type of ring that would result if someone had set a mug of coffee down on it. Only, I hadn't. And neither had Javier. Which meant that someone—or some*thing*—had put a cup of coffee down on the stack of paper between our visits yesterday and today.

"Are you sure it wasn't there before?" Javier asked.

"I don't drink coffee," I said.

"Probably a good thing," said Javier. "You're kind of the nervous type already."

"I am not nervous," I said. "Unless there's good reason. I'm nervous when any halfway intelligent person would be nervous."

"Maybe your aunt did it before she even gave it to you," Javier suggested.

"She didn't," I said. "Look—see where I wrote 'Why a frog?' on the first page?"

"Yes. And it's a good question."

I nodded. "And see how it's a little smeared from the coffee?"

"Uh-huh."

"Well, that couldn't have happened if I had written my note after the coffee cup was placed on the paper. It could only have happened if someone—or some*thing*—put the coffee cup down on top of my writing."

"So," said Javier, "forensically speaking, we have to conclude that someone—or some*thing*—was in the house after we were. Or was still in the house when we left. And that they had another cup of coffee and set it on this particular piece of paper."

"Forensically speaking, yes."

14

"I DON'T THINK *THINGS* DRINK COFFEE," said Javier after a moment's thought. "I'm pretty sure we can narrow it down to some*one*."

"I agree," I said. I'd started to thumb through the pages. "Because *things* don't tend to write suggestions in the margins of books either, do they?"

I handed Javier page 2 of Caroline's book, where I'd written the stuff about the creepiness and the Presence and where was Grampa?

There was my writing, in the Red Pen of Ideas for Improvement. But there was more writing underneath it. A lot more. In black ink.

Javier read aloud what the black ink said: "'What about a time vortex? Grampa could have been imprisoned in a time vortex by a powerful warlock. That would explain why the house looks as if it has been empty for a while.'" He looked up from the page. "A time vortex. That's a cool idea."

"Right? Keep going."

"'Perhaps Grampa himself is a warlock and has lost a battle with a more powerful (and evil) foe.'"

"Foes always work," I said. "Everyone likes a powerful foe in a book. Especially an evil one."

"They do," Javier agreed. Then he read, "'Gerald, naturally, will have to rescue his grandfather from the evil warlock's vortex.'"

Which was sort of like my storm drain idea, only ten times better.

"So then what happens?" Javier asked, flipping quickly through the pages. "How does it end?"

"They get a prize for biggest zucchini at the county fair," I said.

"No way."

But now that he'd come to the end, Javier saw that it was true. The Black Ink of Excitement didn't go past the second page. Gerald and Grampa still wound up with just a big zucchini for their troubles.

"That's disappointing," said Javier.

"No kidding. But whoever wrote this has some good ideas. If Caroline goes for these suggestions, maybe she can put in the rescue herself, and that would change the ending."

"What if Grampa doesn't grow vegetables in his garden?" said Javier after a moment. "What if he grows other, way more interesting plants? Magic plants. Because he's a powerful warlock."

"That makes sense," I said. "What self-respecting warlock would grow vegetables? Here." I handed him a pen from his desk. "Write that down."

He did. Then he looked up. "This is good stuff," he said.

I nodded.

"One thing, though," said Javier.

"Yeah?"

"No way is Gerald a frog."

15

"YOU HAVE TO SALT THE WATER," I reminded my mother that night. "It's your only chance to season the pasta."

"Stop hovering," she said. "You're in charge of dressing, remember?"

I backed off, but not before tossing a palmful of salt into the pot on the stove. Three summers ago, when some child-care plans fell through, I'd spent a lot of time with my grandma Sally. She didn't cook, but she was a huge fan of cooking shows. I learned many things that summer, number one among them the importance of salt.

"I saw that!" my mother snapped. "Caroline and Lu are here— go let them in."

Caroline and Lulu were having dinner with us. Caroline came inside carrying a fresh stack of paper and looking pleased with herself. Lulu, on the other hand, looked a little off. She said being pregnant was making her queasy.

Caroline and my mother took their places side by side at the kitchen counter and started chopping salad ingredients— both using the same poor knife technique. They were lucky they still had twenty whole fingers between them.

I went back to work on my famous lime vinaigrette.

Lulu came into the kitchen as I was emulsifying—a crucial, sometimes tricky step in making dressing where you combine the oil and the acid (in this case lime). "Alex!" she said. "Can I see you for a minute?"

I finished whisking first—you can't rush the emulsification process, as any cooking-show veteran knows—and nodded.

Lulu grabbed my upper arm and pulled me into the living room. "Thank you for helping Caroline with her book," she said when we were alone. "It means so much to her. I think she was more freaked out by what the agent said than she let on. I was starting to be sorry I'd gotten involved."

"Sure," I said. "It's kind of fun."

"She was really inspired by your suggestions," Lulu said. "She stayed up late rewriting the whole first scene to make it more—ominous? That was your idea, wasn't it?"

"I was thinking creepy, with some danger. Danger in a book is like salt in food," I went on like I knew what I was talking about. "You need to add some to make it interesting."

"Right. Although can we not talk about food?" Lulu begged. "I think that's what she's done. She won't show it to me, though. She wants to get your approval first."

I was weirdly pleased to hear that.

"Anyway, I want you to know that I think you're a great nephew and you're going to make a great cousin!" Lulu pulled me into a hug, which I didn't love. "And now if you'll excuse me," she said, "I'm going to sit outside on the porch where the smell of food can't reach me."

And she practically ran out the front door.

16

THE NEXT PERSON TO GRAB ME by the arm was Caroline. Why were the aunts so grabby this evening? I hoped it wasn't turning into a trend—my arm was going to get all stretched out and not match the other one.

"Alex," she said, dragging me toward the sofa. "I'm so excited about the new beginning for the book."

"Great," I said as she sat and yanked me down next to her. I took my arm back and kept it close by my side.

She ran her hands through her hair, pulled it into a ponytail, then let it go again. "The only thing is . . . ," she began. Ponytail, unponytail. "Now that I have the creepy beginning and the Presence with the capital *P* and the missing grampa . . ."

Ponytail, swirling around into a bun, unbun: She was going to be bald by the time this conversation was over. On the plus side, my arm was safe.

"I know," I said. "Where do you go from there? I've given that some thought."

"You have?"

"I have notes. I'll go get them."

"Um, okay, sure."

I ran upstairs and came back with my copy of the book.

She left her hair and my arm alone while she read the notes on the first pages.

"Alex, these sensory details are incredible!" she said. "The cobwebs, the creaky floors . . . You have quite an imagination."

I smiled modestly.

"It's funny how your handwriting changes when you change pens," she said.

I was caught off guard by this. She thought all the ideas written on the pages were mine, naturally. Who else's would they be? I couldn't tell her they included major contributions from a coffee-drinking ghost or maybe cleaning person. That was way too complicated. "Huh?" I managed.

Fortunately, she didn't pursue it. She was busy reading. "A vortex and a warlock . . . That's definitely a new direction. But . . ." She reached toward her hair and then changed her mind. "I just don't know if it's my style." She studied me for longer than was comfortable. Finally, she said, "Will kids your age go for a supernatural twist like that?"

"Sure," I said. Did she not watch TV?

"That *would* solve the problem of the missing grampa. And making him a warlock in his own right—I could do that." She kept reading. Then she said, "I love this about Grampa growing magical plants. . . . What if, instead of a warlock—because I'm not sure you can even *have* a good warlock—we make him a . . . potion master? He grows the magical plants to use in his potions. Would that work?"

"Sure," I said. "And Gerald can rescue Grampa, right? From the evil warlock and the vortex? After a battle of some kind?"

"Gerald has to save Grampa," Caroline said. "That's what happened in the original too."

Was it? I nodded politely.

"But I don't know about an actual *battle*. I don't want it to be too violent. Won't that scare kids?"

She definitely didn't watch TV. Or see any movies either.

"I'm pretty sure it won't," I said. "But you could put in some other nonbattle stuff for him to do—you know . . ."

"Trials!" said Caroline. "Tests of intelligence and character."

"Yeah," I said. Although I'd been thinking more along the lines of cool adventures and heroic deeds. I hoped she wasn't going to assign math problems and community service to poor Gerald.

She grinned at me. "Oh, and Alex?" she said.

"Yeah?"

Her shiny pink fingernail tapped the first page of the book and my original note about "Why a frog?"

"Already taken care of," she said. "Gerald is no longer a frog."

That was a relief.

"And the zucchini?" I had to ask, bracing myself.

"Compost," said Caroline.

17

ON MONDAY AT SCHOOL, JAVIER AND I described our weekend to Marta over lunch. Marta had broken her elbow trying to do a handstand on her skateboard Saturday, and her arm was in a sling. At least the purple sling matched the headband she was wearing to hide her bang stubble.

Let's just say this wasn't Marta's first broken bone and it wouldn't be her last. Marta was the director of Javier's video series of stupid stunts. She was also the star. Technically, she wasn't allowed to spend time with us due to some past filming accidents and a strict mother, but Marta didn't live her life based on technicalities. And, besides, she couldn't get hurt at lunch. We hoped.

"I can't believe you guys broke-and-entered without me," she complained.

"We didn't break," I objected. "We only entered. With a key. And you were grounded."

"I would have come in a heartbeat and you know it," she said. "So do you think the house is really haunted?"

"Maybe," I said, just as Javier was saying, "Of course not."

"We think it was a cleaning person who likes coffee," I admitted.

"And literary criticism," said Javier, without looking up from carefully removing the corn kernels from his vegetarian chili and placing them in neat rows on a napkin.

"They weren't criticizing, they were making suggestions," I said.

"Same thing," said Javier. "If it was already perfect, no suggestions would be necessary."

"True," said Marta, her mouth full of Javier's rejected corn. "My mom ish conshtantly making shuggestions about my choishes"—here she swallowed, thank goodness—"and don't think for a second that she isn't criticizing."

We'd met Marta's mom. She was definitely criticizing.

"So we have to go explore the haunted house, right?" said Marta. "Preferably at night."

"We aren't going back," I said, just as Javier was saying, "Not at *night*."

Marta rolled her eyes long and hard. Neither of these responses was what she'd been looking for. She'd been looking for something like, *Of course we're going back! At the stroke of midnight! And to make it extra fun, we won't bring our phones or even a flashlight!*

"I'm going with you next time," she said. "I'll put together a kit of ghost-hunting stuff."

"Don't you mean cleaning-person-hunting stuff?" said Javier. "You know, maybe a couple sponges we can set out as lures?"

"You're hilarious," said Marta. "You're also a complete dud."

"So did your aunt take all the suggestions?" Javier asked me.

"The ones in the margins? What about my magic-plants idea?"

"She was totally excited about all of it," I said. "She's going to use the warlock and the vortex and the magic plants and send me a new version as soon as she's done."

"What about the frog thing?"

"Taken care of."

"Zucchini?"

"Zilch."

"Well, okay, then."

18

CAROLINE CAME THROUGH—SHE MUST have stayed up all night again writing—and there was a new version of *Gerald Visits Grampa* (we were going to have to make some "suggestions" about that title) in my e-mail that afternoon. It was a lot shorter than it had been before, because she'd lopped off the middle and the end. I printed out a paper version for myself and e-mailed copies to Javier and Marta, who wanted to read it too.

Marta texted me before I'd even started reading the new version.

We can do this, she wrote.

I texted back the classic question mark.

(I'm going to write the texts down here as if we were saying them, because writing them the way we texted is too complicated. Marta used at least six different emojis for "dud" alone, depending on her mood.)

The roof. We can get him down.

Gimme a sec, I texted.

I read quickly. Caroline had done a good job—this was way less boring than the original version. Grampa's house was creepy, and there were some hints at danger, the feeling of a Presence. And the sensory detail was really working. All this I had expected. But then my aunt surprised me.

When Gerald couldn't find Grampa anywhere, he started searching the house. And as he did, the house starting disappearing. Room by room, it vanished, leaving a misty void. And who doesn't enjoy a misty void in a book? No one, that's who.

Gerald had to scramble to get away from the void, and he ended up on the second floor, climbing out a window and onto a porch roof. Where he was stuck, because the whole inside of the house was now gone, though the outside was mysteriously intact.

That's where it ended. The last line, which was written in a different font and, I figured out after a moment of confused staring, wasn't part of the book, said:

"How do I get him off the roof?"

That's what Marta had been texting about. Getting Gerald off the roof. And if anyone knew how to get someone off a roof, it was Marta. There was only one problem. Marta's experience leaving roofs tended to involve a long drop followed by a painful bounce.

Okay, done, I texted Marta and Javier. **How do we get him off the roof?**

What about a tree limb? Marta wrote. **He could grab a tree branch and swing to the ground like a monkey.**

Too predictable, Javier texted back immediately.

Plus, Grampa is a gardener, I wrote. **He wouldn't let a tree branch grow so near the house.** My dad was a total nut about trees near the house, so I knew what I was talking about.

Geez, said Marta. Okay, what about a drainpipe? He could slide down a drainpipe.

Not sure he could really do that, Javier texted. They are attached to the side of the house.

How do people do it in movies? Marta asked.

How do people do anything in movies? said Javier.

How do people do anything in books? I asked.

I thought this was a good point, but both of them ignored it.

Trellis? said Javier after a few moments of standoff. We have a trellis on the side of our screen porch. Maybe he could climb down it like a ladder.

That wasn't a bad idea. But Gerald was a boy now, not a frog. He was a lot heavier than he used to be.

Would a trellis hold him? I asked.

Naturally, it was Marta who replied: Only one way to find out!

19

So there I was the next afternoon, sitting on the roof of Javier's porch, staring at the top of the trellis and thinking about gravity. The trellis looked downright flimsy. And how was it anchored in the ground? I couldn't tell from this angle, and we hadn't checked before I got out here.

Javier and Marta were in Great-Aunt Rosa's room, which had a window over the porch roof. The window I'd crawled out of. Great-Aunt Rosa wasn't home, conveniently for us.

Javier was filming me.

Marta was coaching me.

"It's easy," she said. "Just inch yourself down the slope on your butt. No need to stand up."

There was no way I was standing up on the roof, and I think that should have been clear to everyone already.

It turns out that roofs that don't seem steeply pitched or high up when you look at them from the ground are completely different when you're on top of them. When you're on top of them, they feel like a waterslide and a high dive combined. Except without any water to land in. And that was a crucial difference, now that I thought about it.

When Marta had suggested a human trial for the trellis question, she had been thinking of herself as the stunt person, of course. But when we got to Javier's house, she had to admit that even she couldn't crawl out the window and then climb down the trellis with her arm in a sling.

So it was up to me.

I sat there on the porch roof, trying to take in as much sensory detail as possible while I had the chance. The late-afternoon sun on my face. The gritty shingles under my hands. The icy trickle of fear pooling in my knee and stomach areas. Part of this pause was for the book, but most of it was plain stalling.

"Alex, it's going to be dark soon," said Marta. "Get a move on!"

"All right, all right," I said.

I hitched my way down the roof on my butt as Marta had suggested. When I got to the edge, where the trellis leaned against the house, I tapped the trellis with one foot, trying to test how sturdy it was. It felt solid—it wasn't one of those plastic ones. So that was good. What wasn't good was what Javier said next.

"Wait there!" he called. "I've got to run downstairs and film from below for the rest."

Which left me in an almost literal cliff-hanger situation.

20

I **WAITED ON THE EDGE OF** the roof for Javier and Marta to get into place on the grass below me. I was starting to think they'd stopped for a snack when I heard the back door bang shut.

"And . . . action!" said Javier when he was ready, and he and Marta chuckled.

I needed to face the house as I climbed down the trellis. This meant that I had to roll over onto my stomach on the roof and feel around for places to put my feet in the trellis. None of this was flattering when I saw the recording later. Javier certainly wasn't trying for any glamour shots from down there, and I certainly wasn't providing them from up here.

Once I found my first footholds, I shimmied down the roof on my stomach until I could find two lower footholds. And so it went until I was almost off the roof and ready to grab hold of the trellis with my hands.

"How is this thing anchored?" I called.

"Anchored?" said Marta, which wasn't encouraging.

"I want to make sure it's not going to tip over when I put all my weight on it," I said.

"I'll hold it," Marta offered.

Marta didn't weigh as much as I did, even before you factored in the weight of the trellis, so this didn't reassure me in any way.

"Don't lean back," said Javier. "Keep your center of gravity forward."

Now I was basically clinging to the trellis like Spider-Man, except without the sticky hands and feet. Or the self-confidence.

"You got this," said Marta from her position below me.

And I did. Sort of. For a while, anyway.

I clambered slowly down the trellis, trying to keep my center of gravity forward, whatever that meant. I was just relaxing enough to think about sensory detail when one sound in particular got my attention.

It was the sound of the trellis cracking beneath my left foot.

21

FORTUNATELY, I WAS MORE THAN HALFWAY down when I fell. Unfortunately, I fell awkwardly and landed funny on my hand. It didn't hurt that much until I got a look at it. The index finger was bent way farther back than any finger should ever be. As soon as I saw that, it started to hurt a lot.

Marta noticed it and screamed. Which was strange, because Marta could basically see her own blood jetting out of her in pulsing spurts and laugh. But faced with an injury not her own, she fell apart. So on her list of career options: stuntwoman yes, doctor no.

I was lying on the grass, cradling my injured hand and fighting the urge to puke, when a shadow loomed over me. It was a long shadow because it was late in the day, not because the shadow's owner was tall. Which she wasn't.

"What seems to be the problem here?" Great-Aunt Rosa asked.

"Alex broke his finger off," said Marta.

"And where is it now?" asked Great-Aunt Rosa.

"Where is what?" asked Marta.

"The finger."

"On my hand," I said.

"So you didn't break it *all* the way off."

"It might be dangling by a thread," said Marta. "Or a tendon or something," she added, to make it sound more medical, I guess.

Great-Aunt Rosa knelt down on the grass next to me, being careful not to kneel on the hem of her skirt. She took my injured hand in both of hers. "The finger is completely attached," she said, turning my hand over gently. "But it is sprained. Wait here." She got up and headed for the house.

"Is she going to call an ambulance?" asked Marta. Marta was familiar with most of the EMTs in the area and had certain favorites.

My stomach—already queasy, to use Lulu's word—lurched. I had a horror of calling 911. I could have been lying squashed under the wheels of a tractor trailer and still be croaking, *No 911*. But that's another story.

"No one needs to call an ambulance," I said. "I'm feeling better already."

"She's getting the first-aid kit," said Javier.

"I hope it's the Deluxe First Responders' Kit," said Marta, who apparently had favorites among first-aid kits as well. "The Standard isn't going to do it with something as ghastly as this."

22

GREAT-AUNT ROSA MADE DO WITH THE Standard first-aid kit, in spite of Marta's grumbling. She did a really good job of bandaging my finger into a normal position, as a matter of fact.

When she was done, she gave me back my hand and asked, "Better now?"

"Much," I said. I was sitting up and feeling less nauseated. Especially since 911 was off the table.

She nodded.

"Thanks!" I remembered to add as Great-Aunt Rosa walked back toward the house. She waved without turning around.

She hadn't asked what had happened, though maybe she had seen the broken trellis and figured it out. But she hadn't asked *why* it had happened either, which most grown-ups usually did.

"How is she so good at bandaging?" I asked Javier.

"She used to be a nurse in, like, the Crimean War," he said.

"The Crimean War?" I repeated. "Wasn't that Florence Nightingale's war?"

"I was jok—" Javier began, at the same time that Marta said, "Did your great-aunt meet Florence Nightingale?"

And again I asked myself how it was that we all went to the same school and had such different levels of information.

"So did you record all that?" I asked Javier.

"Right up until you fell," he said. "I'm not that cold."

"I guess Gerald could use a trellis to get off the roof," I said.

"Part of the way, at least," said Marta.

"So that problem's solved," I said. "I'll let Caroline know."

I stood up and decided I was okay to walk home, even though my finger was still throbbing under the bandage and my whole hand felt eight times bigger than usual.

I'd made it partway down Javier's front walk when he yelled after me, "We need to get you into better shape if you're going to find your grampa."

And Marta added, "You can do it. You just need to push past the pain."

23

IT FELT WRONG WALKING INSTEAD OF running home from Javier's, but I couldn't bring myself even to jog with that gigantic, throbbing Disney-character hand hanging from my arm.

It took way longer to walk home than it did to run. When I finally got there, I explained the injury to my mother as the result of a freak pogo-stick accident. This wasn't a complete lie, but that accident had happened two years ago, and I wasn't that badly hurt at the time. Neither Javier nor I had even looked at his pogo stick since then. They aren't as fun as they appear to be.

After dinner that evening, typing with most of my fingers, I wrote Caroline an e-mail describing the trellis and how Gerald could use it to get off the roof. I didn't mention any falling or spraining. I made Gerald seem pretty graceful and athletic.

She wrote back almost immediately.

Great solution! Of course Grampa would have a trellis. I have an idea, though. To make it more exciting, I'll have Gerald get partway down and then fall. It would be more interesting to make him a bit of a klutz in the beginning, right? Then readers will be rooting for him as he gets more coordinated later on.

A bit of a klutz? Really? Obviously, I'd made the whole thing sound way easier than it had been. But I comforted myself with the idea that Grampa's trellis would have to be extra strong to support his magic vines or whatever, so it wouldn't just snap under Gerald as he made his way down. Gerald, unlike me, would *have* to be a bit of a klutz to fall from Grampa's sturdy trellis.

About an hour later, a new version of the book came from Caroline. She was a fast writer, that was for sure. She'd added the scene with the trellis and the fall. All good. But there was a new cry for help at the bottom:

"Where do I go from here? How on earth is Gerald going to find out about the vortex, let alone rescue Grampa from it???"

I didn't have an answer for that one.

Neither, it turned out, did Javier or Marta at lunch the next day. Getting a person off a roof is one thing. That was something we could try out ourselves and record and describe. Okay, there'd been a minor accident, but my finger was already almost fine. Getting Gerald from the bottom of a trellis all the way to a warlock's vortex was way harder.

"This is a whole plot turning point," Javier said, picking the raisins out of his oatmeal-raisin cookie. "Isn't that the writer's job? To come up with plot turning points?"

We agreed that it was. Ordinarily.

"But," I said, "we're the ones who sent Caroline off on the whole vortex thing—she was thinking gardening and county fairs."

"Don't remind me," said Javier.

"Wait a minute," said Marta, after we'd sat there thinking about the boringness of prize zucchinis for a while. She threw a handful of Javier's raisins into her mouth. "Washn't it the ghosht who came up with the vortexsh idea?" She gulped down her raisin clump and chased it with a swallow of milk. "And that was a huge plot turning point, right?"

She was right. The last big plot turning point had been the ghost's idea.

"So?" said Marta, way too eagerly.

"So what?" Javier and I said at the same time.

"So let's ask the ghost what happens next!"

24

I STILL HAD THE KEY TO the Old Weintraub Place, so it wasn't impossible to "ask the ghost" what should happen next. And since it wasn't impossible, for Marta it was merely a matter of badgering before Javier and I agreed to try.

We decided we would go over that afternoon and casually drop off the new printout. Leave it there on the kitchen table and go home, and come back the next day to see what had happened. If the ghostwriter (which is what we were calling it now) wanted to contribute, it could.

We met at Javier's house. I had the key and the book. Javier had his camera. Marta had a suspiciously full-looking backpack.

"What is in that thing?" Javier asked her.

"Ghost-hunting supplies," she said. "As promised."

"We aren't trying to hunt any ghosts," I said. "We're just dropping off this stack of paper and leaving. Right?"

"Right," Javier said.

"Sure, whatever," said Marta.

When we got inside the house, Marta put the backpack down and started rummaging around in it like Mary Poppins. She pulled out an ancient TV antenna thingy that she'd obviously scrounged from her basement and stuck foil balls on the tips of. She looked proud of it—much prouder than she should have.

"This will tune in to any ghostly activity," she claimed as she lengthened the prongs as far as they would go.

"It's not even going to tune in to any TV activity," Javier said. "Unless you want a show from the seventies."

"What's it supposed to do if it tunes in to a ghost?" I asked Marta.

"Vibrate, maybe," said Marta. "Or hum. Possibly dip." The antenna dipped as she said this. "I did that on purpose," she added quickly. As if Javier and I would have thought otherwise for even one second. "But it will probably do something like that if it detects anything. It's never been tested in the field before, so we won't know for sure until it happens."

Nothing happened, of course. We made it into the kitchen without detecting even the ghost of a centipede.

I set the stack of paper on the kitchen table. There was a Post-it sticking out of the last page, where Caroline's question was. I had put it there myself. It had a red question mark on it, so the ghostwriter would know where to look.

Javier and I were ready to leave. But Marta had gone to visit her backpack in the front hall and returned with some kind of makeshift miner's hat on her head. On closer inspection, it was a plastic souvenir batting helmet with a flashlight duct-taped to it. What was left of her curly hair was sticking out around the helmet, making her look like the deranged clown from every kid's nightmares.

"This'll take a few minutes," she announced, swishing her antenna like a sword in front of her.

"What will?" Javier asked.

"Our exploration of the basement," said Marta, yanking open the nearest door. "Come on."

25

MARTA WAS HALFWAY DOWN THE BASEMENT stairs when she noticed that neither Javier nor I was following her.

"Get over here!" she yelled.

"We'll wait until you're done," said Javier, pulling out a kitchen chair and getting ready to take a seat.

"Don't be such a dud," said Marta. "I need you to film in case something goes down."

Javier sent me a look that suggested the only thing going down was his opinion of Marta's grip on her marbles. But he picked up his camera.

"Let's go," he said to me.

"You don't really need me to—" I began, but he cut me off.

"You first. I'll film you both, just in case."

"Just in case what?"

He didn't reply.

Marta was well into the basement by the time Javier and I joined her there. I wasn't even thinking about the sensory detail. Grampa's house was all void inside now, so there was no basement for Gerald to explore. Still, I couldn't help but notice that this was a basement-basement, rather than a rec-room-basement: dim, musty, and chilly.

I stood near the bottom of the stairs, and Javier filmed half-heartedly while Marta scurried around with her ridiculous hat and antenna, looking for who knows what.

Then she found it.

"Guys," she said, "come here. I think we know who our ghost is."

"We" didn't have a ghost as far as Javier and I were concerned. But the two of us wandered over anyway, because we knew we weren't getting out of the basement until we had.

"Check this out," said Marta triumphantly. She kept blinding us in turn with her headlight as she looked from me to Javier and back again.

"It looks like a bunch of cardboard boxes," said Javier, shading his eyes with his hand.

Marta had one of them open.

"Hey," I said, "there's trespassing and then there's . . . opening people's boxes of private stuff."

"We're not being nosy," said Marta. "This is an important clue. The boxes say 'Rob's Books' on them, and look what's in this one."

We looked. The box was full of—surprise!—books. Fat paperbacks, to be exact.

"So?" said Javier.

"So Rob is, I'm guessing, the late Mr. Weintraub," said Marta. "And these were his books."

"The late Mr. Weintraub had a lot of books," Javier observed.

"A lot of a specific type of book," said Marta. "Science fiction and fantasy. And you know what science fiction and fantasy books are full of, right?"

I shrugged. Reluctant reader, remember?

Javier just filmed patiently, waiting for whatever this was to be over so we could leave.

"Time vortexes," said Marta. "And warlocks. Our ghostwriter is the late Mr. Weintraub, the fantasy fan."

26

"**I THINK IT'S 'VORTICES,'**" **SAID JAVIER** after a moment's consideration.

"*What?*" asked Marta in a tone that would have stopped me cold.

"The plural of 'vortex,'" Javier said.

Marta treated him to the full glare of her headlight. He blinked. "None of us," she said slowly, "are ever, *ever* using that word for more than one vortex. Understood?"

Javier and I then had to wait for Marta to "run some tests" on the rest of the basement. She spent a long time with her antenna poked inside the dryer, insisting she was "getting some readings" in there.

"Does that thing detect lint?" Javier asked.

"Lint is full of static," said Marta. "That might explain it. Either that or some ectoplasm has adhered to the lint through some type of electromagnetic . . ."

It went on from there, but I'll spare you.

By the time we got upstairs, Marta was convinced that Mr. Weintraub's ghost was haunting the place, and that he had somehow managed to pick up a pen and write those notes on Caroline's pages. Because why not? What else did he have going on?

Javier was quiet as Marta went on with some further theories about how a ghost would manage a pen, not to mention a cup of coffee. "Maybe he makes coffee out of habit, from when he was alive," she theorized. "He probably doesn't need the caffeine anymore."

I kept expecting Javier the Debunker to break in with a good reason why none of this was possible and how it was a cleaning person for sure. But he didn't. Which was freaking me out. If Javier was starting to buy Marta's ghost theory, what was to prevent me from buying it too? I was way more gullible than he was.

Finally, I interrupted Marta's monologue and said to Javier, "What do you think? Cleaning person, right? Or some kind of vagrant, maybe?" That last one I just chucked in there in case Javier wanted a theory that seemed edgier, to compete with Marta's ghost.

"The thing is," Javier said, "the person who wrote those notes really does have to know about fantasy books." He looked at me helplessly, as if he knew a plastic hat with a flashlight was in his future but he could do nothing about it.

"Cleaning people read," I pointed out. "And vagrants. They must have some time to read."

"That's true," said Javier. "But right now, we can't rule anything out, can we?"

27

WE COULDN'T RULE OUT A GHOST. Which for Marta was as good as having met and chatted with one about time vortexes over a nice cup of coffee. She was practically hopping up and down as she took off her hat and stuffed it into her backpack with the antenna.

"I knew the ghost detector would work," she said. She was fluffing her curls as if she knew instinctively how bad the hat hair was.

"It did *not* work," Javier pointed out. "You found some boxes of books. With your eyes."

"Whatever, dud," said Marta. "I can hardly wait to see what ideas the ghost of Mr. Weintraub comes up with next."

We coasted through school the next day, waiting for the moment when we would walk into the Old Weintraub Place and find the answer we needed, neatly written on the last page of Caroline's book.

We were feeling more at home in the house when we went back that afternoon—we weren't nearly as jumpy as we'd been the other times. Maybe this was because we now believed that whoever was lurking there was a reader of fantasy, so maybe a nerd but not evil.

The book pages looked untouched when we found the stack on the table, exactly where we'd left it. No notes. Not even a coffee ring.

"Well, this is disappointing," said Marta.

"Maybe the ghost needs more time to think," said Javier. "Maybe we're being impatient. It's a big plot turning point we're asking about, not just what color Gerald's socks should be."

I hadn't even considered the color of Gerald's socks. That was an important sensory detail. I made a mental note to come up with something that would suit Gerald. Then I realized that Gerald hadn't been described at all since he'd stopped being a frog. I made a bunch of other mental notes and stuffed them in my messy mental filing cabinet.

"I guess we can give it a few more days," I said.

But it was disappointing.

I sent an e-mail to Caroline when I got home, telling her I was working on the problem but needed some more time.

She got back to me almost immediately. "That's ok," she said.

I've decided to write some backstory while I wait for inspiration to strike. I'm sure you can help me with this— you have such a lively imagination! I need flashbacks showing Gerald with Grampa. Having a conversation or doing something together. So we can see what their relationship is like, and how much Grampa means to Gerald. That way, Gerald's quest to rescue him will gain importance. Any ideas on what they might say to each other would be much appreciated!

This wasn't good. Now Caroline was convinced I had a "lively imagination." Which I didn't. At all. What I had was a willingness to put myself in situations and be filmed in them and take notes on what they were like. That was the opposite of imagination.

The problem with this new task was obvious. I didn't have a grandfather or even an older uncle I could have a conversation with.

28

HERE'S THE THING ABOUT GRANDFATHERS. MOST kids my age had two. Some lucky ones had even more. I'd seen kids with their grandfathers—at parties and soccer games and school events. The grandfathers pretended to steal the grandkids' noses and slipped them cash when their parents weren't looking. They came to games and cheered from the sidelines in folding chairs that they carried around in their trunks for that very purpose. They thought everything their grandkids did was awesome, and if they didn't think something was awesome, they pretended not to notice it.

My father's father died before my parents even got married. My mother's father, Alan, was called Big Al. My mom, Alison, was Little Al. And when I was born, I was Tiny Al. By the time Alvin was born, Big Al had died. That meant Alvin was just Alvin, not Micro Al or whatever he would have been.

So I had a grampa for a few years, but I didn't remember him. There was a framed photo on my dresser of Big Al holding me when I was a baby. And the way he was looking at me, it was obvious that he would have been a great nose stealer. There was barely a nose visible on my face in the picture—I looked like a baby earthworm. Now I had the type of nose a grampa could really get ahold of. And no grampa.

I needed to have a conversation with a grampa, which meant I was going to have to borrow one.

Grampas aren't library books, Javier texted back when I asked to borrow one of his. **You can't take one out for a while and then return him.**

Why not? I asked.

There was a long pause while Javier struggled with my iron-clad reasoning. **Doesn't matter anyway,** he wrote back eventually. **One of mine is on an oil rig, the other two are on a cruise to Alaska.**

Those were the most outlandish excuses I'd ever heard. It was like he hadn't even tried for believable.

Why don't you just claim they're on a shuttle to the space station? I typed.

That is actually where they are currently, Javier wrote back. And even though it was a text, I could hear his huffy voice. Whenever Javier used the word "currently," he was being huffy.

I let him stew for a while, which he hated. Finally he broke. **I have an idea,** he wrote.

I didn't respond. Two could play the huffy game.

Great-Aunt Rosa is always going to the senior center to hang out, Javier continued. **There are probably old guys there you could talk to. Some of them must be grampas.**

Great idea! I wrote. **When can we go?**

29

MARTA HAD NO INTEREST IN GOING to the senior center with us. "That kind of thing doesn't call for my particular skill set," she said.

"If you mean waving antique TV parts around, you're probably right," said Javier.

"It worked" was her only response.

The senior center was a few blocks from Javier's house. Great-Aunt Rosa took the senior shuttle there, according to Javier, but your age had to be in the upper double digits to ride on it, not the extreme lower ones. So we took our bikes.

I'd never been to a senior center before. I'd been expecting some dusty old place, but it looked like a newer, nicer version of our school. Plus, it smelled way better.

There was no one at the front desk, so we walked right by it, toward the sound of voices down the hall.

We passed a room where people were doing aerobics that looked way more strenuous than anything I, for one, could keep up with—and I'm in good shape from all the running. Then we walked by a room where people were playing cards. It might have been poker—it looked fairly intense. Then yoga—ditto. Finally, we came to a bigger room full of tables and chairs, where people were chatting and drinking coffee.

"Where's Great-Aunt Rosa?" said Javier, scanning the room. "She's got to be where the coffee is."

But she wasn't there.

"Maybe she's doing yoga, and she was upside down so we didn't recognize her," I said. But neither of us could picture Great-Aunt Rosa upside down.

"Well, now I just feel weird," said Javier. "I was thinking she could introduce us to some likely grampas."

So there we were, standing around awkwardly, obviously way under the age limit for the senior center. We were bound to attract attention eventually. And sure enough, we did.

30

"EXCUSE ME," SAID A LADY SITTING at the table nearest to us. "Are you lost?"

Were we lost? Would it help if we were? Then the seniors might feel sorry for us and gently send us on our way without asking any awkward questions. Maybe with a couple of those big chocolate-chip cookies from the platters on the sideboard there, if we were extra good.

I was about to say yes, we were lost, when Javier said, "Oh no, we're not lost. Thanks for asking, though." Which was way more mature and honest and polite. But it did leave us kind of dangling.

"Then, can we help you out with something?" the woman asked. She seemed perfectly kind and genuinely willing to help, but that attitude can turn ugly fast if you don't have the right response. I knew that from experience, but that's another story.

Which might explain why I didn't just tell her we were looking for Great-Aunt Rosa. That would have been the logical thing to do, right? But I was so concerned about saying the wrong thing and angering the nice lady that my mind went blank and I punted.

Here's what I said: "I'm, um, I'm here to visit my great-uncle.

His name is . . ." What was a normal old-man name? All the guys I knew were named things like Fletcher and Cooper, and those names weren't going to fly here. "Frank!" I said, happy with my choice. No one under sixty was named Frank. "My great-uncle Frank was going to meet us here this afternoon."

Javier was looking at me like he wished he had his camera because he knew I was only going to dig myself further into whatever hole this was, and he wanted it captured for eternity.

"Oh, sure," said the tall, skinny man sitting next to the helpful lady. "I know Frank. He's a great guy. We can find him for you."

Crud. The old-man name I'd picked was already taken.

"Oh, ah, no, that's okay," I said. "My uncle isn't the Frank who's a great guy. I mean, *I* think he's a great guy. Because he's my uncle and everything. But—"

Javier stepped away from me at this point, like he didn't want what I was suffering from to spread to him.

"Ah," said the man. "'Nuff said." He winked at me. "A different Frank. I get it."

Jackpot! I was thinking now. "'Nuff said" was an awesome grampa expression. Completely authentic. And the knowing wink? Bonus! This kind of detail was exactly what I was looking for. This guy was a gold mine. I needed to keep him talking.

"So, come here often?" I asked him.

31

JAVIER SNORTED. IT WAS THE SAME snort that was frequently heard in the audio of his films involving me. I ignored it, as I always do.

"I come here a few times a week," said the skinny guy. "Mainly for the chocolate-chip cookies, you want to know the truth. Right, Ellen?" He poked the woman's arm and she laughed. "The name's Nate," he said to me. Which was a way better old-man name than Frank. Why hadn't I thought of Nate? "And you are?" he asked.

"I'm Alex," I said. "And this is my friend Javier."

"Nice to meet you, Alfred and Javier," he said.

"Uh, it's Alex."

"Right. Albert."

I hadn't realized he was hard of hearing. I tried again, louder. "A-*lex*," I enunciated.

He laughed. Then he stuck his hand out toward me. I ducked away from him, certain he was going to steal my nose.

"Whoa, there," he said. "I'm trying to shake your hand, not slap you silly."

Slap you silly. Make a note of that, I told myself. "Oh, sorry," I said. "I kind of figured you were stealing my nose. You know— that 'Got your nose' trick people do?"

Nate nodded. "I'm familiar with it," he said. "But isn't that for much younger kids than yourself and your friend here?"

"My friend here" was working hard not to laugh. Trying not to laugh was taking up almost all of his concentration and energy. I didn't have to be looking at him to know this.

"I guess it is," I said. I'd had no idea there was an upper age limit on nose stealing. What else didn't I know about grampas?

Nate moved his hand toward to me once more, slowly and carefully this time. "A pleasure making your acquaintance, Albert," he said as we shook. Then he shook Javier's hand without incident. "Would you boys like to have a seat, maybe try the senior center's famous chocolate-chip cookies?" he asked.

We sat. We ate. The cookies were superb—warm and chewy, with just the right touch of salt, the way chocolate-chip cookies are supposed to be. We left about an hour later, without realizing that no one had mentioned "Uncle Frank" again.

32

JAVIER LAUGHED ALMOST THE WHOLE WAY back to his house. He could barely keep his bike upright. I sort of hoped it would go over, but he was an excellent multitasker.

"Sorry," he kept saying, not sorry at all, between spasms of laughter, "but I had to hold it in for so long, it just built up."

"*Something* built up, all right," I muttered. I had no idea what that was supposed to mean, but it felt good to mutter it.

So we parted annoyed with each other, but I was in a hurry to get back to Caroline with my latest research.

Conveniently, she was in our driveway when I got home, wedging a large box into her small hatchback and fending off Marcello with one foot.

"Is this thing a dog or a rat?" she asked.

"That's kind of an ongoing discussion. Mom and Alvin say dog. Dad and I say rat-dog mix. Heavy on the rat."

Caroline studied Marcello while he yapped intensely at one of her back tires. "Mark me down for team rat-dog," she said. "Seeing this, I'm almost tempted to put a rat-dog hybrid into my book, but . . . yuck."

"I know," I said as Marcello ran off to torment an innocent

pedestrian on the sidewalk. "Who'd want to see something like that in a book?"

"I'm borrowing Alvin's old stroller for the baby," Caroline told me, giving the box a final shove with her shoulder and slamming the hatchback closed. I hoped the baby liked animal crackers, because I had personally seen young Alvin drop more in that stroller than he'd ever managed to put in his mouth. Although knowing Caroline and Lulu, they'd power-clean every nook and cranny down to the molecular level before allowing their child within ten feet of it

"I was at the senior center today," I told her. "I did some research on talking to old men. For Gerald's conversations with Grampa."

"Oh, honey, you didn't have to do that!" she said. "I know what kind of imagination you have. You could have just given me some ideas about how you think it might go."

"I—uh—I could have," I said. "But I don't have any grampas, and I wasn't sure . . ."

Caroline came over and took both my hands in hers. Yes, it was awkward. Then it got worse.

"I'm so sorry, Alex," she said. "That was incredibly thoughtless of me. You've never really known a grampa, have you?" Her eyes got shiny and she blinked a couple times.

"No," I said, gently wiggling my hands out of her grasp, "but I did learn some stuff. First, they don't pretend to steal your nose at my age, so you shouldn't put that in."

"Um. Right. I won't. Thanks."

"And second, they can be hard of hearing. I told this guy my name was Alex, like, three times, and he kept calling me Albert."

Caroline laughed, which was better than the near-crying but more confusing.

"Oh my goodness," she said. "He was teasing you. Dad—Big Al—used to do that all the time to kids. My friends included. He called them all Oscar, even the girls."

Nate had been teasing me by calling me Albert? Was that what they'd all been smiling about around the table? I really had a lot to learn.

Caroline looked up at the sky for a second, then back at me.

"I wish you'd known Big Al. He would have been an amazing grampa." Her eyes were getting shiny again. Now she was sniffling and rummaging in her pockets for a tissue.

"I got lots more good old-man stuff," I said quickly. "Like winking and saying ''Nuff said.' I'll write it all down and send it to you."

"That would be fabulous," Caroline said, dabbing at her eyes with a linty blob of pocket tissue. "This book is really shaping up, and I'm so happy you're helping."

Then she grabbed me by the face and kissed me. 'Nuff said.

33

JAVIER HAD FILM CLUB AFTER SCHOOL on Monday, so I hung around and then we walked to his house together. We were going to meet Marta there after her elbow checkup, then go over to the Old Weintraub Place to see if we had an answer from the ghostwriter.

When we got to Javier's front walk, we could see someone sitting on the porch swing. It was a small person, but it wasn't Great-Aunt Rosa. It was Marta. As we got closer, she jumped up and ran down the porch steps.

"Guys!" she said. "Where have you been? I've been texting and texting."

We looked at our phones. She was correct: She'd been texting Where r u??? over and over again to both of us.

"Javier had film club," I said. "You knew that."

"I guess I did. I forgot in all the excitement."

"Weren't you at the doctor? How was that exciting?"

"I was only there for about two seconds. They say I've been 'moving it around too much' and it's 'not healing as fast as it should be.' They don't know what they're talking about," she said, waving her arms around to make sarcastic air quotes.

"Clearly," said Javier, gently pushing her injured arm down to her side with one finger.

"Dud," she said. "But never mind. Because look what I have!"

She reached into her bottomless backpack and pulled out a stack of paper. Caroline's pages.

"Where did you get that?" I asked. "It's supposed to be at the Old Weintraub Place."

"It was," said Marta. "I got tired of waiting for you, so I went over to conduct some experiments around the outside, just see what kind of energy patterns I could detect."

Javier snorted, and it was good to hear it directed at someone who wasn't me.

"You couldn't wait for us?" I asked. But we all knew she couldn't.

"It turned out the back door was unlocked," Marta said. "So I walked right in."

34

"**WE DIDN'T LEAVE THE BACK DOOR** unlocked," I said. "Did we?"

"Nope," said Javier. "We used the front door."

"Then how could it have been unlocked? It can't have been unlocked ever since Mrs. Weintraub moved."

"Maybe the cleaning person left it open," said Javier.

"I thought we agreed there was no cleaning person," said Marta. "I thought we agreed it was a ghost we're dealing with."

"We did not agree to that," said Javier. "That was never formally agreed to."

"We did," said Marta. "At least Alex and I did. Right, Alex?"

I honestly had no idea what I'd agreed to at this point. "Why did you take the book?" I asked her. "We need to leave it there until we have an answer."

"Why do you think I've been texting till my thumbs are stubs?" Marta said. "We do have an answer. And I think you're going to like it."

"You already read it?" I asked.

"Of course I did. I've been sitting out here in the cold forever! I needed something to read."

"Let's see it," I said.

She handed the pages to me, and we sat down on the porch steps.

"Read it out loud," said Marta.

I did. "'When he fell from the trellis, Gerald accidentally entered a slipstream that leads to an alternate world. His grandfather created the slipstream to move between the two worlds. The warlock followed him from the alternate world into this one, where he captured Gerald's grandfather, then covered his tracks with the void. The time vortex where the grandfather is imprisoned is in the alternate world.'"

"Doesn't that sound good?" said Marta. "I have no idea what a slipstream even is, and I'm still all in with it."

"A slipstream is an area of low pressure behind a fast-moving vehicle," said Javier.

"How does he know that," I asked Marta, "if we don't? When did you learn that?" I asked Javier. "Were we out sick that day?"

He just smiled and shrugged.

"So, is a slipstream the same as a vortex?" Marta asked.

I left that one to Dr. Dictionary.

"Not really," said Javier. "A vortex is more like a whirlwind. That's why you can get trapped in a vortex but slide through a slipstream. It makes sense if you think about it."

Did it? Enough, I guess. Marta was nodding, anyway.

I went back to reading the note. "'The grandfather's house in the alternate world is intact—the void hasn't crossed over—but it is different from the original: It is the house of someone with magical powers. And the inhabitants of this world are not all human. In fact, most of them are not.'"

"That opens up some possibilities," said Javier.

It did, but I had no idea how I was going to interview gryphons or elves or whatever else the ghostwriter had in mind. Grampas were enough of a challenge.

"Read the last part," Marta said.

"I'm getting there," I said. "Don't rush me.

"'Gerald can use the magical resources in the alternate house to rescue his grandfather,'" I read. "'As long as the warlock doesn't know he's there.'"

35

"HUH," I SAID WHEN I WAS DONE.

"Huh," agreed Javier.

"'Huh'?" said Marta excitedly. "Do you see where the ghost-writer is going with this? This turns the story into a real fantasy with an alternate world. Like the books we saw in the basement," she said. She let that hang a moment for effect. "The books belonging to a ghost. A ghost named Rob," she concluded. She sat back like a lawyer who had just proved that her accused client's pet hamster was the murderer.

"Maybe . . . ," said Javier slowly. "Maybe . . ."

"Maybe what? Speak up," said Marta. "Maybe what?"

Javier ignored her hectoring. "Maybe Rob isn't Mrs. Weintraub's dead husband. Maybe he's her son, and he's secretly living in her old house because he lost his own in a fire, or he gambled it away, and now he doesn't have anywhere to go but—"

"Sorry," I said. "Mrs. Weintraub only has a daughter. I know that for a fact. From my mom."

"A daughter Roberta?" asked Javier hopefully.

"Melinda. And Mrs. Weintraub lives with her."

"Oh, well. I tried."

"You did try," said Marta. "But you failed."

Javier took his defeat pretty well. "Fine," he said. "I give up with the rational explanations. All aboard the express train to Ghostville."

"Yes!" said Marta, and she made a bunch of train-type noises that don't deserve a description here or anywhere else.

I knew Javier wasn't really on board the express train, and neither was I. There were still any number of reality-based explanations for the notes on the book pages. And Javier and I could discuss them as much as we wanted—as long as Marta wasn't around. When Marta was around, we would ride along in her slipstream. Or maybe swirl around in her vortex.

It was just easier that way.

I stood up and put the pages in my backpack. "I'm going home," I said. "I want to send these ideas to Caroline as soon as possible."

"It's not an organ for transplant," said Javier. "I think it will last until you get there."

"I don't know," said Marta. "It seems like the heart of the book to me."

She wasn't joking.

"In that case, I'll get a cooler," said Javier.

He was.

36

I WAS EAGER TO SEND THE ghostwriter's ideas to Caroline when I got home, but fate, as they say, had other plans.

My mom was on her phone when I walked in the door. "How's he doing?" she was saying. "Do they know what it was?" She looked over at me and grimaced.

That's how I knew this had something to do with Alvin.

"Okay. Let me know when you can," she said, and ended the call.

"Your father and brother are at the doctor," she told me.

"What now?" I asked.

I really was curious to hear what had happened. Because with Alvin, it was always interesting.

Alvin was a voracious reader, as I've already said, but his reading didn't make him wise or keep him out of trouble. In fact, the opposite was true. He liked to think of himself as a scientist, but mainly what he experimented on was himself. And the results often led directly to the doctor's office. Let's look at it this way: Marta put herself in danger because she thought it was fun and had no understanding of gravity. Alvin did it because he was curious and had no understanding of cause and effect.

He also seemed to believe that the holes in his head were interchangeable. Here's one of many available examples: He had to go to the doctor twice in the same day when he was five. The first time, he had shoved a minimarshmallow so far up his nose, he couldn't get it out, and the second time, he had eaten an unknown number of cotton balls. Several objects have also been pulled from his ears. I'm guessing there are still things inside his head that he hasn't bothered to tell our parents about.

"He was making his own sunscreen," said my mom.

"Out of what?"

"That's what we need to find out. Something he's allergic to, anyway. His skin broke out in blisters."

"Where?" I asked, not really wanting to know.

"Only his arms, thank goodness." And then she added the Alvin refrain: "It's a good thing he's cute."

It was hard for me to admit it, being his brother, but Alvin was ridiculously cute. And that had probably kept my parents from leaving him at the doctor's on one of their many visits. He was nearsighted, like my mom, and wore tiny kid glasses that made his brown puppy eyes look even huger. I got Mom's nose. Full size. Alvin had one perky cowlick. I had so many, I looked like I'd been mauled at a petting zoo.

"Do you want me to make dinner?" I asked. Mom tended to burn things when she was distracted.

"Would you? I'm going to search his room for whatever he was experimenting with up there."

I was pulling out the ingredients for tacos when I noticed that the economy-size cayenne pepper jar was almost empty.

"Mom?" I yelled up the stairs.

"Yeah?"

"I think I know what caused the blistering."

37

DINNER WAS READY WHEN DAD AND Alvin got home.

Both of Alvin's arms were wrapped from wrists to pits with gauze, and whatever ointment the doctor had used on them had a funky odor. Dad said he looked and smelled like someone had been called away in the middle of mummifying him.

"Do we have any gauze?" Alvin asked as we ate our bland, cayenne-less tacos. "And maybe some unguents as well?"

"Why?" Mom asked him warily.

"I was thinking that I could finish mummifying myself."

Dad put down his fork very, very gently. "Alvin . . . ," he began, in a soft but in no way patient voice.

"Never mind."

So it was a long evening before I sat down with the ghostwriter's newest plot twist, ready to type it up and send it to Caroline. I opened the pages to the note. And that's when I realized that the note didn't end with "as long as the warlock doesn't know he's there." The paragraph ended there. But the note went over onto the back of the page. Apparently, the ghostwriter hadn't planned what it was going to say before starting to write and had run out of space.

Marta must not have seen the last part of the note when she read it herself, because she hadn't jumped down my throat and ordered me to finish after I'd stopped at what I thought was the last sentence. And she definitely would have wanted me to read the rest.

"When Gerald lands in the alternate world, he's injured," the note on the back of the page said. "And there to aid him are two creatures. One is an imp called Snarko. The other is the Daredevil. Snarko has a magic spyglass that lets him see the truth about things. The Daredevil cannot be hurt, with the exception of her elbows. If she is struck in the funny bone, she falls unconscious for several hours. The two agree to help Gerald navigate the alternate world and find his grandfather.

"It's important," the note said, "to have trusty sidekicks on any quest."

Okay so far. But there was one more part of the note. And this was the part that threw me. It threw me pretty far, to be honest. And I think I might have landed on my head.

Here's what the last part of the note said:

"When Gerald opens his eyes after the fall from the trellis, Snarko the Imp and the Daredevil are standing over him. He doesn't believe what he's seeing at first. He thinks he simply fell into his grandfather's garden. But gradually he realizes that he is no longer where he started out.

"Snarko says to him: 'We need to get you into better shape if you're going to find your grampa.'

"And the Daredevil says: 'You can do it. You just need to push past the pain.'"

Which, if you're keeping track, is exactly what Javier and Marta said to me after I fell off the trellis.

I don't think I would have needed the last two quotes to understand that Snarko and the Daredevil were based on Javier and Marta. It was clear from the descriptions. Actually, it was clear from their names.

But something far creepier was also clear. When I fell from the trellis, we were at Javier's house. The three of us were alone when Javier and Marta said those things. Well, okay, yelled those things. But not loud enough for someone all the way over at the Old Weintraub Place to hear.

This meant that the someone—or some*thing*—from the Old Weintraub Place had been in or near Javier's yard when I fell. Was it a cleaning person who had followed us to Javier's and hidden in the bushes while I climbed down the trellis? Not possible, since we hadn't been to the Old Weintraub Place the day I fell.

Was it a vagrant who lurked in Javier's neighborhood, sometimes having coffee at the Old Weintraub Place and sometimes hiding in Javier's shrubbery in case anything interesting happened? Possible, but highly unlikely.

Or, and this was where I'd been headed all along: Was it the ghost of Rob Weintraub, who sometimes got bored at his own house, so flitted around the neighborhood just for kicks? Was it a ghost that could, if it chose, *follow us home*? I already ran everywhere—I really didn't want to have to start sprinting.

That last theory was a first-class, one-way ticket aboard the express train to Ghostville. Which is where I ended up, right there at Ghostville Station, holding my luggage. And if you'd looked into that luggage, you would have seen an old TV antenna and a stupid hat with a flashlight duct-taped to it.

38

ORDINARILY, I DIDN'T WELCOME surprise visits from my brother as I was getting ready for bed. Or any other time. He was cute, sure, but he was also a little brother and by definition a pain. Tonight, though, I was coming to terms with a new belief in roaming ghosts, so I was glad for some company when Alvin arrived.

"How are your arms?" I asked him. "Still hurting?"

He shrugged. "Not really."

"What made you think hot pepper was a good sunscreen ingredient?"

"The big sun on the label," he said as if I were an idiot. "There's a big sun on the label, which implies that the contents are accustomed to being in the hot sun. Which means that they have sun-protecting capabilities."

If you're thinking that I am writing words here that eight-year-old Alvin didn't really use at the time, think again. This was truly the way he talked. Maybe all those words he gobbled up when he read had to spew out when he spoke or his brain would overheat. Or something. That was my theory, anyway. You're welcome to offer a better one.

Alvin's logic was off, but not all the way off, if you think about it.

"That big sun on the label means the pepper in the jar is hot," I said. "Like, spicy hot. Not that the peppers themselves are sun-proof."

"They should be sun-proof, though," said Alvin. "They grow in the sun."

"Wouldn't that make almost all plants sun-proof?" I asked.

"Maybe they are. I've only just started experimenting."

"Well, take my older-brother advice and don't try poison ivy next."

"You're hilarious," he said. Then he noticed Caroline's pages, still open to the ghostwriter's note. "What's that?" he asked, walking over to my desk.

My first instinct was to throw the nearest item of dirty clothing over the book and blurt, "Nothing!" But what was the point? He'd already seen it. And it wasn't like it was a secret book or anything.

"It's a book Aunt Caroline is writing," I told him. "She wanted me to read it."

"Can I read it?"

Could he? I mean, obviously he *could* read it—faster than I could. But did he have permission to read it? I had no idea. But he was my little brother, which easily decided the matter for me. I didn't want Alvin elbowing his way into Caroline's book with his voracious-reader ideas. This was *my* project.

"I think Caroline wants me to read it first," I said. "She'll probably ask you when she's done. She'd want it to be perfect before you read it."

He was scanning the visible page now with his hungry-shark eyes, gobbling words in big gulps.

"Okay," he said. "I can wait."

Which was way too easy, looking back on it.

39

I MANAGED TO TYPE UP THE new ghostwriter ideas and e-mail them, along with my full grampa-conversation report, to Caroline before I went to bed. My actual homework was still in my backpack, untouched.

I didn't like the idea of the ghost of Rob Weintraub floating around town, taking note of our conversations, but I kept reminding myself that so far he seemed harmless and even helpful. Just another book and coffee lover, like any customer at the bookstore café downtown, except ectoplasm based. And he couldn't help that, could he?

I was too tired to text Javier and Marta about Snarko the Imp and the Daredevil that night. So it was lunch the next day when I told them, which means I told them in person and was able to see their responses.

Marta shrugged. "Shoundsh good to me," she said through an enormous mouthful of pasta salad.

"What sounds good to you?" I asked.

"Two shidekicksh. One can shee the truth, the other can fight her brainsh out without getting hurt. That'll work, right?" she said and somehow swallowed at the same time.

I glanced at Javier, waiting for him to tell Marta that (a) Snarko and the Daredevil were based on him and her, and (b) this clearly meant that the ghost of Rob Weintraub was the one helping us with the book.

Instead, he stared back at me blankly, his eyes unfocused. He looked like he'd been replaced by his identical but much dumber twin.

"Javier?" I said, snapping my fingers in front of his face. "Do you have a response to this?"

His eyes refocused, thank goodness. The blank stare had been disturbing.

"Snarko the Imp?" he asked.

"He's you, right?" I said. "I mean, the Daredevil is Marta and Snarko is you." I desperately needed someone to back me up on this.

"And he's an imp," Javier said, still not helping.

"Yes. You know what an imp is, right?" I asked him.

I was hoping he did, because I wasn't sure myself. I knew in general, of course. But if he wanted a dictionary definition, I didn't have one.

(Then. I do now. Here it is: "imp: a small demon: fiend. A mischievous child: urchin." Here we were dealing with the first kind.)

"Yes, I know what an imp is," said Javier. He took a bite of pasta salad with a green pepper chunk still visible inside it. I waited for him to spit the intruder into a napkin, but he didn't. He chewed it, and then he swallowed it. Which wasn't right at all.

But maybe a bit of vegetable was what he needed, because

smart-twin Javier returned from wherever he'd been. I could see his intelligence snap back into place. I let out a sigh of relief.

"So what you're wondering is how did whoever wrote this know exactly what Marta and I said to you after you fell off the trellis?" Smart Javier asked.

"That's exactly what I'm wondering," I said. I didn't hug him and I never would, but I kind of wanted to at that moment.

"Can shomeone pleashe exshplain to me what you're talking about?" said Marta from behind a spray of orange Jell-O.

40

"THAT'S RIDICULOUS," MARTA SAID when I'd finished explaining how A logically led to B.

"Thank you!" I said. If Marta thought the ghost thing was ridiculous, then I could definitely put away the old Humpty Dumpty night-light I had been forced to plug in last night. "So what do you think is going on if the ghostwriter isn't a ghost?"

"Oh, it's definitely a ghost," said Marta. Crud. Back to Humpty Dumpty. "What I mean is, it's ridiculous that you duds think the Daredevil is me. My elbows are *not* weak spots."

"Your elbow is broken," Javier pointed out.

"That's only because I fell on it."

"Which is how things get broken."

"It's one of the ways."

"It's the primary way."

I wasn't sure why Javier was chasing this particular rabbit so far down its bottomless rabbit hole. Usually he gave up a lot quicker and just changed the subject.

"Um, guys?" I said. "Can we go back to the issue here?"

"The *issue*?" said Marta. "Did you say 'issue'?"

"I can say 'issue.'"

"You really can't. Only Javier can say 'issue.' And only *very* rarely," Marta added, giving Javier the side eye.

"I never say 'issue.'"

"Oh, I think you do, my friend. I think you do. . . ."

And here is where our lunch period ended. With absolutely nothing solved or even really discussed, and my two friends acting as if they'd agreed to hold hands and jump off the Cliff of Remaining Sanity together.

It made my trip to Ghostville seem positively normal in comparison.

41

I WENT RIGHT HOME AFTER SCHOOL, partly because I had to do yesterday's homework on top of today's fresh load. But also because I was eager to hear what Caroline thought of the new plot twist from the ghostwriter.

Sure enough, there was an e-mail from her. But it wasn't at all what I had expected.

First, she thanked me for the grampa research and said she was definitely going to use it. Then things went south fast.

> Thank you so much for the ideas about the slipstream and moving into an alternate world. You are so imaginative! And you clearly know your fantasies. I thought your mom said you were a reluctant reader, but she must not count those. What a snob!
>
> I'm afraid that I'm not nearly as comfortable creating an alternate world as you are, though. This feels like a giant leap out of my comfort zone as a writer, and I'm afraid it would show. I did try! I wrote up the scene with the new characters. But I think I'm going to go

back to the original after Gerald falls from the trellis. He'll wake up and his grampa will be there, and the whole void thing was a hallucination he had as a result of hitting his head in the fall.

I feel like I'm on firmer footing with the gardening plot (no pun intended). But I think the changes in the beginning will really draw the reader in, so thanks for all your help with that! I'll be certain to give you your well-earned money when I see you next, and throw in a bonus too!

As a PS, she added: "Not to worry—Gerald still isn't a frog!"

Oh no was all I could think. What a disappointment. Javier and Marta were going to be so bummed. But not as much as I was. As I sat there in front of this depressing e-mail, I realized how much I'd been enjoying thinking about this book. And collecting sensory details and ideas for it. And even reading the new parts as she wrote them. I wanted to know what happened next, especially now that there was an alternate world and inhuman sidekicks involved.

And what about the ghostwriter? What was our ghostwriter going to do without this hobby? Hang around heating up coffee and waiting for trespassers to eavesdrop on? What kind of afterlife was that?

I had no idea how to respond to Caroline's message, so I closed it and figured I'd come up with something polite later, when I'd had a chance to digest the news. Which was going to be hard—I hate zucchini.

42

I GOT MY HOMEWORK DONE AND went to bed without plugging in Humpty Dumpty. It was weird, but my worry about a ghost had faded. The ghost seemed to have been part of the whole Gerald fantasy, and now that we were back to prize zucchinis and "It was all a head injury" (Really, Aunt Caroline? The old *Wizard of Oz* movie trick? I thought you were better than that), I was back in real life without even a ghost to liven things up.

I had texted Javier and Marta with the bad news before I went to bed. I'd been lying there for a while in the dark when my phone buzzed.

The text was from Marta, to me and Javier. It said:
Nooooooooooooooooooooooooo!!!!

Then one came from Javier. It said: Bummer.

Then Marta: Maybe we can keep going ourselves!

Javier: We're not writers.

Marta: We could be!!!!

Me: We really couldn't.

Javier: Maybe you can convince your aunt to change her mind.

Marta: You have to!!!

Me: Stop using so many exclamation points!!!

Marta: You are a complete du

And nothing more from her after that, because her mother had taken her phone away. This happened frequently after bedtime. I'm surprised her mother didn't just confiscate her phone every night. But theirs was a strange relationship.

Then, after a while, during which I almost fell asleep . . .

Javier: Frog?

Me: Nope.

Another pause.

Javier: Zucchini?

Me: Yup.

Javier: Shame.

Me: Yup.

And that was the end of that for the night.

43

WE WERE SOMBER AT SCHOOL THE next day. Marta suggested going back to the Old Weintraub Place that afternoon, to "scare" the ghost, as she put it. "To see if it can be done," she said. Which was a little bit intriguing but not enough to lift our sagging mood.

Javier had a film club meeting, though, and he didn't want us to scare any ghosts without him. So I ended up going for a long run. Just to blow the smoke off myself, as my mom would put it, quoting Big Al.

My run ended up at the senior center. I'm not sure why I went in; I could have run by it and kept going. Or circled around it and gone home. Maybe I wanted a chocolate-chip cookie. Maybe I wanted to be called Albert again, now that I knew it was teasing. This time I could roll with it, as if I'd been in on the joke all along.

There was no one at the desk when I went in. Security in this place wasn't tight, that was for sure. But based on the workout I saw going on as I headed down the hall toward the room with the cookies, I was pretty sure the seniors could take on whatever they had to. I peered around the doorway into the cookie room to see if anyone I knew was there.

Sure enough, there were Nate and Ellen and their friends Bill, Henry, and Lucy—sitting at the same table they'd been at last time. Same chairs, too, as far as I could remember. I knew they'd moved in the meantime, though, because they were wearing different outfits. Except maybe Henry.

"Hey, Albert!" said Nate when they'd seen me hesitating in the doorway. "C'mon over and take a load off."

Take a load off. Good one. Except now I didn't need any fun old-man sayings, did I?

"Cookie?" Ellen offered.

"Take two," said Lucy. "They're just out of the oven and at their peak."

I took two and bit into one. Lucy was right. It was perfect.

When I was done chewing and swallowing, I said, "Do you always sit in the same places when you come here? Is it like the cafeteria at school? Are there cliques?"

"I suppose there are," said Ellen. "But we're not exclusive."

"You're not?"

"We let you in, didn't we?" said Henry. "And you're not only new, you're also quite a bit younger than we are."

"Also sweatier," said Nate.

"Sorry about that. I ran here."

"Why?" asked Nate. "Was something chasing you?"

"No," I said. "I just don't like to walk when I can run." True enough, but that was another story.

"Ha!" said Nate. "Albert, you are a stitch and a half."

Stitch and a half. Maybe Caroline could use some of this good stuff in her new/old version of the book. Maybe a more lively grampa would make it more interesting. Or at all interesting.

"Albert, you look depressed," said Nate. "What's on your mind?"

I shook my head, not believing it myself. "A book, actually."

"It must not be a very good one."

"It could have been," I said.

44

THERE WAS SILENCE AROUND THE TABLE. Which felt like my fault. I took another bite of cookie and tried to nudge the conversation away from the book that could have been.

"So," I said, "do you like to read?"

Everyone around the table laughed.

"Sure we do," said Ellen. "Who doesn't?"

I shrugged like I had no idea and what a wacky notion not liking to read was!

"What kind of books do you read?" I asked the table in general.

"Historical fiction," said Ellen. "Preferably British. With beheadings."

"Cookbooks," said Lucy. "Except when I'm hungry."

"Thrillers," said Bill. "Cold War, mostly."

"Military history," said Nate. "Civil War is my favorite."

"Large print!" Henry finished.

They laughed again.

"What about you, Albert? What do you like to read?" Nate asked.

"Me?" I swallowed the last bite of my first cookie. I knew that no matter what I said there would be awkward follow-up questions, so I opted for the truth. "Um. Not much. I'm what they call a reluctant reader."

"Who calls you that?" asked Nate. "Sounds like a load of cow flops, if you'll pardon my French."

Cow flops. Pardon my French.

"If you ask me," said Ellen, "you just haven't met the right books yet."

"It can take time," said Lucy. "Like meeting the right man." She looked over at Bill and smiled. He smiled back.

"Lucy," said Nate, "you are a hoot."

A hoot.

"But I think Ellen's right, Albert," he said to me. "You need to keep trying. Someday you'll meet a nice book and fall head over heels."

This was getting confusing. Were we even talking about books?

I had the distinct feeling I was being teased again.

45

YOU KNOW HOW WHEN SOMETHING BAD happens, you just want your life to go back to the way it was? And if it does, it seems improved: Your old, ordinary life seems better compared with the badness. Well, it turns out the opposite can happen when something interesting happens. If that goes away and you get your old life back, the old life seems duller. It's like putting your old sneakers back on after you try on new ones.

I wandered through the next few weeks not appreciating much of anything. Even the weather was gray and wet, which meant a raincoat on most days, which meant an extra layer of insulated sweat when I got home from school. Which is what my mother immediately objected to one Friday afternoon when I got inside the house.

"Alex, you need to shower," she said soon after I got my coat off. Insultingly soon, really. "We're going to Caroline and Lu's for dinner."

When we got to Caroline and Lulu's house, Caroline had a strange look on her face. Like she'd accidentally eaten a bug and couldn't decide if she'd liked it or not. *Conflicted*. That's how she looked, if you want a one-word description.

She made a grab for my arm, but I was ready for her and dodged it. So she grabbed me by the ear instead. Which was painful and made me regret that I hadn't let her at my arm. She led me into her "office," which was a broom closet with a small desk in it instead of brooms.

"So, this is where the magic happens," I said when she'd let go of my poor ear.

"Yup," she said. "Have a seat."

I sat down on a pile of printer paper boxes. She sat in the swivel chair in front of the desk and swiveled around to face me. I rubbed my sore ear and waited for whatever was going to happen.

"I need your help," she said.

Eep. Was there another book on the horizon? *Gerald Visits Great-Aunt Letitia*? What if she was planning a whole series of visits with increasingly uninteresting relatives? What if *Gerald Visits Grampa* was the action-packed one of the group?

"Okay," I said. "With what?"

Her hair was up in a bun already. I could see her hand reaching for it and coming back frustrated. She tucked nothing behind her ear and said, "With my new book. *Gerald in the Warlock's Weir*."

46

THERE WAS A LOT IN THERE to deal with, and I started with the simplest question. "What's a weir?"

"It's like a dam. D-A-M. In a river."

"I know what a non-swear dam is."

"Sorry. The non-swear dam is where I'm going to hide the vortex. Mostly because it sounds good as a title."

"Okay. But I thought you'd given up on warlocks and vortexes."

She sighed. "I did. But then I changed my mind."

"Why?"

"Well, that's an interesting story," Caroline said. "But it boils down to one very determined person named Lulu, who went behind my back and sent the version of the book I'd given up on to her friend the literary agent."

"That seems bold," I said. "Were you mad at her?"

"Yes, I was. Sort of. For a while. Until the agent e-mailed me and said she loves the new direction the book is taking and she definitely wants to see it when I'm done."

And now the look on her face told me that yes, she'd eaten a bug, and it was crunchy and delicious.

"She loves it?" I said. "The warlock and the potion master and the vortex?"

"And the alternate world and the sidekicks and my plan for the trials and the rescue. She says that stuff is very popular now, and if I can finish in the next few months, she's pretty sure she can sell it." A big smile crept up her face. "Can you believe it?"

"Sure," I said. "It's a great idea for a book. Even I wanted to read it, and I'm a reluctant reader."

"Pish," said Caroline. "Your mother has no respect for genre fiction."

I had no idea what she was talking about. Writer stuff, I guessed.

"She never has," I agreed as vaguely as I could.

"So I'm going to need you to keep coming up with those great ideas and imaginative details," said Caroline. "And we're talking about a lot more than ten dollars."

We were? That sounded good to me.

I was smiling back at her now. Not because of the money, although that was fine too. I was happy because the book was going forward again. Because my old-man sayings would be useful. Because now I had to find a weir and get a good look at it.

Then I replayed the conversation in my head and asked, "Can you finish a whole book in a few months?"

"I'm going to have to," she said. "Babies are notoriously bad at sitting around and waiting for you to finish a chapter before you feed them. But I write fast and I'm super motivated. It shouldn't be a problem.

"The first thing I need from you," Caroline concluded, standing up, "is a list of whatever fabulous fantasies you've been reading."

Uh-oh.

"I've got a lot of catching up to do!" she said.

47

ALVIN AND I SPENT MOST OF the evening at Caroline and Lulu's crawling around the floors to see if we got rug burns and how many breakables we could find at baby level. Alvin went above and beyond by chewing on an electrical cord, but he wasn't shocked. Just yelled at by both aunts and both parents.

There was a very short break for dinner, after which Lulu made us get back to work. Caroline was right about her—she was determined. She rewarded our hard work by letting us each put a hand on her stomach to feel the baby kicking. It felt more like someone was flicking her from the inside, in my opinion, but I guess if your feet are the size of a pinky finger, your kicking is going to feel more like flicking.

"That's our cousin in there," said Alvin. He got down close to Lulu's stomach and suddenly yelled, "Hellooooo, Cousin!"

"Never do that again," said Lulu.

When we got home that night, I texted Javier and Marta the news that the book had risen from the dead, but we didn't really discuss it until Monday at lunch. Even Javier didn't know what a weir was, so that felt good. Then we got down to the real business.

"How am I going to tell Caroline what books I've been reading when I haven't been reading any?"

"That's easy," said Marta. "We leave a note for the ghost, ask what books it's been reading."

"We don't need to do that," said Javier as he carefully removed walnut chunks from a brownie. "We can go back to the basement and look in the boxes."

"Oh, goody," said Marta. "Let's make the process as dull as possible."

It wasn't that I hadn't thought of going through the books in the basement. I had. The problem was:

"But those are books for adults. Caroline is writing for kids, and she wants to know what kids' books I've been reading."

"Couldn't you tell her you've been reading adult books?"

"I'm way out on a limb with kids' books already," I said. "I don't think I could convincingly claim that I've been reading those big fat adult books."

"You know what you have to do," said Javier. "You just don't want to do it."

"What?" asked Marta. "What does he have to do? What doesn't he want to do?"

But I knew.

"The library," I said. "I have to go to the library."

"Oh, it's worse than that, my friend," said Javier with real pleasure. He sat back in his chair, pointing his moth-eaten brownie at me as he spoke. "You have to ask the librarian to recommend some fantasies. And then you have to sit down. And then you have to read them."

He laughed long and hard, and what was left of his brownie fell on the floor.

48

I PUT OFF THAT TRIP TO the library for days. I kept telling myself I had too much to do after school, but I was mostly lying to myself about that. Finally, on Saturday, I ran out of excuses, so I laced on the old sneakers and ran to the main branch.

It's not like I'd never been there before. I knew the way. I just hadn't spent as much time there as, say, Alvin had. I went in the late afternoon, hoping there wouldn't be a bunch of tiny kids having story hour or whatever they did in the children's room in their waist-high gangs.

The children's librarian was sitting at her desk. She was a get-right-to-the-point type of person—that was obvious from her no-nonsense glasses. And she knew her stuff. She was always recommending books for Alvin that he immediately devoured in his sharklike way.

"Alex Harmon," she said when I'd arrived at her desk. "I knew you would come."

So that was odd, right? It sounded like the kind of thing you'd hear from someone wearing a burlap robe with a hood that hid most of her face. In reality, she was wearing normal clothes, though her sweater looked handmade.

She stared at me patiently. She didn't blink. Her hands were folded in front of her on the desk. They were the calmest, least fidgety hands I'd ever seen.

I felt like I'd arrived at some mystical person's cave after a dangerous trek up a steep mountain. I was surprised she didn't serve me some weird tea made from roots. She did have some normal-looking tea of her own, but she didn't offer me any.

"How did you know I would come?" I asked when the staring had gotten uncomfortable. "I didn't even know I was coming till this morning."

"I've been expecting you," she said.

Which was not an answer to my question.

I was starting to think maybe I'd go to the branch library, when she added, "You're ready, aren't you?"

"For what?" I fought the urge to back away from her slowly and then make a run for it by zigzagging through the picture-book section. I'd have to hurdle over the dad sitting on the floor cushion with his toddler and a book, but I was fast—I could make it.

The librarian smiled. But it was more a smile of satisfaction than cheerfulness. She looked like a predator that has spotted its prey limping across the grassland, wearing thick glasses and a sweater vest.

"What is it you seek?" she asked.

49

"I'M, UH, SEEKING SOME BOOKS," I said to the librarian. I realized I was speaking in the soothing voice my mom used with her high-strung pet-sitting clients. But it didn't seem to work on librarians.

Her smile disappeared. One of her eyebrows rose while the other remained where it was. This is harder to do than it looks, I learned later in front of the bathroom mirror.

"Some fantasy books," I added quickly. "Whatever is good, whatever kids my age like. That's the kind of book I need."

The eyebrow moved back into position. I let out a silent sigh.

"I think I can give you some guidance with that." She stood up. "Come."

Still sort of robe-and-sandals-in-a-remote-cave, wasn't it? Where was her long, knobby staff? I followed her into J Fiction.

"We don't shelve science fiction and fantasy separately in the children's room, but I can make a few suggestions to get you started," she said as we entered the closest fiction aisle.

I was relieved to be in more standard-librarian territory here. At least she hadn't told me I had to answer three questions or battle the Beast of the J Fiction section.

"Three questions first," she said, not one second after I'd had this thought.

"Okay," I squeaked. At least she hadn't threatened me with some sort of abyss if I got any of the questions wrong. Though an abyss seemed like a good idea for one of Gerald's trials, come to think of it. I wished I had one of those stubby library pencils and a scrap of paper to write that down.

"First, child or adult protagonist?" she asked me.

I didn't know what a protagonist was. It sounded kind of painful. "Uh, child?" Gerald was a child, and so was I, so I figured that was a safe choice.

She nodded. I'd passed the first question.

"Second, future Earth or alternate world or something in between?"

At least I got the general idea about this one. "Alternate world," I said.

She nodded again. One more question to go. I had actually broken a sweat at this point. I reminded myself that the children's room didn't have an abyss. Alvin would have fallen into it if it did.

"Third, humorous or serious?"

This one I wasn't sure about. Was *Gerald in the Warlock's Weir* meant to be funny or serious? It seemed fairly serious so far, what with the evil warlock and the grampa trapped in a vortex. But then there were Snarko and the Daredevil. They were funny, especially when they argued. What sealed it was the knowledge that I was going to have to read these books.

"Funny," I said. "Funny would be good."

50

YOU MIGHT HAVE RECOGNIZED SOME ASPECTS of Gerald's climb up the Mountain of Mists to seek the wisdom of the Lost Librarian in the previous scene. If you've read Book 2, that is (and sorry about the spoiler if you haven't). But we were still a long way from the Mountain of Mists when I ran down the library steps that afternoon.

I looked back, once I'd made it partway down the sidewalk, just to make sure a great winged reptile hadn't launched itself from the library roof to come after me, talons spread and jaws wide open. A pair of sparrows on a window ledge chirped at me, but they didn't even bother to fly away as I passed.

I skirted a nearby manhole cover, in case the Beast of J Fiction actually *lived* in the abyss and this manhole was its preferred exit. I found a safe-looking bench and sat for a minute to look at the books.

The librarian had given me three of them, and they were not thin. I wasn't dreading reading them, exactly, but it felt like I had added several more loads of homework to my weekend tonnage.

When I got home, I decided to get it over with. I poured myself a tall glass of lemonade and lay on my bed with the shortest of the three books. I figured I would read the flap, maybe the first chapter, and skim the rest if I got bored. This was basically how I tackled any book assignment.

The flap was fine. Told me what I was getting into without giving the whole plot away. (There's nothing more annoying than "But then a sudden tragedy . . ." in book descriptions. It forces you to spend the whole time waiting for someone—or someone's pet—to die.)

The first chapter was only three pages long, which I appreciated. It ended with a cliff-hanger involving some creepiness and danger. Which proved that my instincts about how to start a book were right. I kept reading. And it kept being interesting and also got funny when the sidekick kicked in.

I managed to read four chapters before my right leg got twitchy and I had to go for a run. As I ran, I compared what I'd been reading to Caroline's book. *Gerald in the Warlock's Weir* wasn't quite as funny as this one, but it was just as exciting. And I might have been biased, but I thought Caroline's sidekicks had more personality.

I came back from my run seriously planning to keep reading. I took a seat and picked up the book. But then I saw my phone lying on the bed. I hadn't checked my messages since before my run. What if someone had been trying to reach me? What if someone had posted something hilarious?

I picked up the phone and started scrolling. There was nothing interesting there. But now the idea of reading a book wasn't that appealing. I sat down at my computer and settled in for some Forehead-level Pimple Patrol.

51

I DID FINALLY FINISH THE FIRST of the books the librarian had recommended. And I read the flaps of the others. Then it was time to return them.

I sent Caroline an e-mail with the names of the books. I felt bad that I hadn't read more than one of them, but in my defense, I'd had a lot of homework during that time, and I didn't feel like recreational reading on top of that.

She wrote back almost immediately.

Thank you soooo much for these!! I will run out and buy them right away. I'm so glad to have you advising me, Alex. You are definitely getting a big shout-out in the acknowledgments when this book is published. Which it looks like it might be!! The agent said she would 'love to represent it' if the ending lives up to the beginning. Still lots of work to do, but your book recommendations are going to be a huge help, along with the fabulous imaginative details you've been providing.

This was all great for Caroline. But it left me in an uncomfortable position. First, she was convinced I was some kind of imaginative genius, when I wasn't. And second, now she thought I'd read all these books and could give her advice on hers. I was digging myself deeper and deeper into this pit of—not lies, exactly, but something close. Something definitely worse than simple misunderstandings.

Caroline had the wrong idea about me, and I was doing nothing to correct that. The fact was, I was having fun working on this book, and I didn't want her to stop asking for my ideas. And she would stop if she realized what I actually had to offer. Which was close to nothing at all.

I looked around at the pit I had dug myself into. And I made a decision: I wouldn't dig anymore if I could help it, but I wasn't ready to emerge from the pit shouting the truth about myself either. That could wait until Caroline was done. Then I would tell her everything. And she could decide if she still wanted to put my name in the acknowledgments. Whatever they were.

52

I WAS STANDING KNEE-DEEP IN A cold stream. I was wearing tall rain boots (borrowed from my mother—yes, embarrassing), but water had long since filled them, so now they were acting as extra-gravity boots. I was holding a large rock in two hands. I had already dropped a similar large rock on my left foot, so I was cradling this one as if it were explosive.

Javier was standing on the bank of the stream, filming me and smirking at me at the same time. Marta was next to him, yelling instructions at both of us. Her elbow was supposedly healed, but her mother still wouldn't let her use that arm.

The stream was small—maybe four feet across—but it made up for size with its coldness. It was also surprisingly deep.

"You can't leave any spaces between the rocks!" Marta yelled.

"They're rocks," I yelled back, "not bricks. There are going to be spaces."

"It's not going to work if the water can go between them."

"It's not going to work if I come over there and bash your toe with this—"

But I couldn't finish my threat, because now I was losing my footing on the streambed and flailing around for balance while holding a large rock. The rock fell, splashing me in all the places I wasn't already soaked.

"I'm going to get pneumonia," I yelled.

"You can't get pneumonia from being cold," said Javier. "That's a myth."

"I can get angry from being cold," I said.

"This was *your* idea!"

It was. I was the one who had decided we needed to know what a weir looked like. And after a bunch of googling, I had given up on finding one nearby. Then I'd had a brain wave. I googled "how to build a weir." And here we were. Two of us warm and dry on the bank of the stream in the woods behind the library, and one of us chilled and soaked and toting boulders, trying to pile them high enough to cause the water level to rise and then spill over.

I had moved seven rocks into place, and was realizing that I needed about seventy more, when I tripped over a submerged branch and fell. I banged my tailbone hard on one of my weir rocks, then rolled off it and into the water.

53

JAVIER PROBABLY KNEW EXACTLY HOW LONG a person could survive in cold stream water, but I didn't. Maybe it was minutes. Maybe it was seconds. I was certain it wasn't hours. I thrashed around in the stream, trying to get my hands under me so I could kneel and then stand up. Everything in the stream was slippery— either hard and slippery and impossible to get a grip on or soft and slippery and too icky to get a grip on.

Finally, I got my hands beneath my chest, only to have them slide sideways, leaving me facedown in the water. Which felt even colder now that my head was under as well. I can swim fine, but swimming wasn't going to help here—there wasn't enough water to float in. But somehow there was enough to drown in. Go figure.

Have you ever heard the expression "It's better than a poke with a sharp stick"? Maybe only my dad uses it. Well, drowning in two feet of water was definitely worse than a poke with a sharp stick. Until I was being poked with a sharp stick in addition to drowning. Which was definitely worse than either one alone.

I grabbed the stick and felt it yank me sideways, which is when I realized that this was not a random stick—it was someone's idea of rescuing me. My hands were so cold, it was hard to hang on, but I did, and I was pulled to the side of the stream, where I lay beached, coughing and shivering.

"Are you okay?" Marta asked.

"Yes," I managed as I crawled onto the bank. "But I might puke."

Marta backed right off. She was a domino puker—if one person started it, she was bound to be next.

I coughed for a while without puking. Then I sat up and peeled off my wet sweatshirt. Javier handed me his without a word, and I used it to dry off as best I could, then put it on.

"Should've brought towels," I said through clacking teeth.

"Who knew you'd be going for a swim?" said Javier.

I emptied the water out of my mom's boots, put them back on, and stood up. "I guess that's enough research for today."

Marta was holding the sharp stick upright beside her like a spear. Had she really pulled me out of the stream with one arm? There was something not quite human about that girl. She pointed the stick at me and said, "You didn't finish your weir."

Javier reached over and guided the business end of the stick toward the ground. "I think we have what we need," he said.

54

IT WAS A SUNNY DAY, SO I dried off quickly as we walked toward my house from the stream and its feeble attempt at a sloppily built weir. As I warmed up, though, I realized how badly I'd hurt my tailbone on the rock when I fell. I was walking like an old man, and that meant I wouldn't be running anytime soon.

Marta was still carrying the stick, and neither Javier nor I was up for asking what she planned to do with it. Sometimes it was easier to stay in the dark.

"That could have gone better," I said finally.

"At least you got a feel for it," said Marta.

"A slippery, cold, wet feel for it," I said. "Not to mention a pain-in-the-butt feel for it."

"You know," said Javier, "most times when a person says, 'I think I'll write a book,' the next thing you say isn't 'Uh-oh, someone's going to get hurt.'"

"True," said Marta. "It's not like when someone says, 'I think I'll go cliff diving without any lessons—I can figure it out on the way down.'"

Javier nodded. "And it's not like when someone says, 'I've got a terrible itch I can't reach. I think I'll roll around in broken glass—that should take care of it.'"

"It's not like when someone says, 'You know what's really holding back my trapeze career? The safety net. That thing has to go.'"

"It's not like when someone says, 'I lost my glasses, but I can still find my way down the black-diamond slope no problem.'"

"It's not like when someone says—"

"I get it," I broke in. "Writing a book isn't supposed to be dangerous. But I'm not writing a book. I'm researching details for a book to make it realistic. By trying things out. And sometimes that turns out to be dangerous."

"I don't think fictional-character stunt double is an actual job," said Javier. "And I'm pretty sure your aunt never hired you to be one, even if it is."

He was right. Caroline would have been horrified to see me falling off that trellis or flailing around in that stream.

"As soon as my mom lets me use my arm again, I'll take over," said Marta. "Because I'm thinking that fictional-character stunt double might be my dream job."

55

ALMOST A WEEK AFTER THE WEIR incident, just as my tailbone was feeling like itself again, I got home from school and encountered my dad looming in the front hall.

"Alex," he said. "You want to see something strange?"

"Is Alvin involved?"

"No—it's not something that's been in his nose. I promise. It's even stranger than that. Something you hardly ever see. Something you may never have seen before."

"Geez, Dad, just show me," I said. I had stuff to do.

He walked me into the kitchen and pointed dramatically at the house phone.

"Look at that," he said.

I looked. And it *was* strange. The base under the phone had a tiny screen on it, and that screen was lit up with a number 1.

"Ever seen anything like that before?" my dad asked. He was enjoying himself.

"What does it mean?"

"It means someone called—on the house phone. And they left a message."

"Who would do such a thing?"

"That's where it gets even more interesting," said Dad. "The message is *for you*."

That didn't make any sense at all.

"What do I do to get it?" I asked.

"You press play," said my dad. "And then you listen."

"How do you know it's for me?"

"I already listened to it."

"Then why can't you just tell me what it said?"

"Well, first of all, because this could be your only chance to listen to a message left for you on a landline. It's historic! And second, because I want to see the look on your face when you hear it." He folded his arms and leaned ever so casually against the wall.

So now I was picturing all kinds of stuff. A famous movie star asking me to play him as a child in an upcoming movie? A contest that I'd won without knowing I'd entered? A teacher calling about a paper I wrote that was so awesome, she had to . . .

But my dad's face didn't have "something cool for Alex" written all over it. Or even "something impressive Alex did." My dad looked interested. And amused. So this was probably more along the lines of "something embarrassing about Alex."

I pressed play.

56

THE MESSAGE WAS SHORT and to the point.

"This is a message for Alex Harmon," it began in a woman's no-nonsense voice. A familiar no-nonsense voice. "I'm calling to inform you that the book you require is waiting for you at the library. Thank you for your prompt attention to this matter."

My father was outright grinning now. That huge grin that showed all his teeth and then some.

"I have no idea what this is about," I said.

"You didn't reserve a book from the library?"

"No, I didn't. Maybe this is for Alvin."

"She said Alex. Quite clearly."

"So what do I do?"

"Sounds like you'd better hustle on down to the library and pick up the book you require."

My father was still grinning as I went out the door.

I arrived at the library as most people were leaving. I went over to the checkout desk and told the lady there that I had a book waiting for me.

She looked around the reserve shelf for a while, then asked me to repeat my name. She searched some more and gave up.

"Sorry," she said. "When did you get the message? Maybe it's gone back to the stacks if it's been a while."

"I got the message today," I said.

"Do you know who left it?"

"The librarian from the children's room."

"Well, it's possible she has it, then. Why don't you run in there and check?"

Of course. Of course this would involve going back to the librarian in her remote alpine dwelling.

I could have left at that point. But I was my father's son: curious. Plus, I'd come all this way. Plus, my dad was not going to let up if I came home without an explanation for the historic Message on the Home Phone.

So I thanked the lady at the desk and headed up the mountainside to the lair of the librarian.

57

THERE SHE WAS, SITTING AT HER desk, waiting like a well-read spider for the fly (me) to bumble onto her web looking for a book it never requested.

"Alex Harmon," she said when I arrived at the desk. "You got my message, I take it."

What, exactly, was she taking and where?

"Yes, but I don't think I requested a book."

She studied me, and the dried sweat from my run reliquified in my armpits.

"You read only one of the three books I recommended last time you were here," she said.

Okay, how did she know that?

I didn't ask that question out loud, but apparently she had psychic powers—maybe she got them from tea she brewed from old bookmarks.

She rested her hand on a book lying on her desk. "I know when a book comes back read and when it doesn't," she said.

She looked me up and down. I started to wish that the abyss I'd been trying to avoid last time would open so I could dive into it, Beast or no.

"Were they not what you needed?" she asked.

"Um, no, not at all. I mean yes, yes, they were. What I needed. They were great. It's just that I, uh, I didn't have time to read all of them."

"And?"

Looking back on this conversation, it occurs to me that the librarian would have made a great police detective. The library was getting ready to close, but she was staring at me like we had all night if that's what it took. So I spilled. Gushed, pretty much.

"And I got restless and I went running and my phone pinged and . . ."

She held up a hand, and I ground to a halt before I got to ". . . I had to pee a few times."

She turned in her chair and pulled a plastic box off the shelf behind her. "This is for you," she said.

I took the box from her. "This isn't a book."

"It most certainly is a book," she said.

I wasn't going to argue. If she said the box was a book, then the box was a book. And if she wanted to tell me my big toe was a book, I was going to take my sneaker and sock off and sit down right there and try to read it.

"I look forward to hearing what you think," she said.

And I was dismissed.

58

THE BOX CONTAINED A LITTLE DEVICE, I found when I opened it outside the library. A little device you could plug earbuds into. Thinking there might be some top-secret spy-mission instructions recorded on the device for me, I started listening right there on the sidewalk. What I heard was not secret instructions, but the opening lines to an audiobook. The book was one of the librarian's recommendations that I'd returned unread. She'd given it back to me in audio form.

I had a twenty-minute run home, so I decided I might as well give this book a twenty-minute try. I didn't know if the librarian could tell if an audiobook had been listened to, and I wasn't going to take any chances. Next time she'd probably try giving it to me in Braille, and I would be in big trouble then.

My dad used to read to me, and then Alvin and me, before bed every night when I was little. He still read to Alvin sometimes, and I admit that I usually listened from across the hall while pretending not to.

My dad grew up in Bermuda, and he had an unusual accent, which made his reading even more enjoyable. (Though Alvin and I would never admit that, and made fun of his pronunciation of certain words.) The author of the book I was listening to as I ran home from the library was British, and so was the narrator of the audiobook. Not quite the same accent, but it reminded me of my dad's.

The best thing about the audiobook, though, was that I could listen and run at the same time. I didn't like to listen to music when I ran because I couldn't hear what was going on around me, and someone could come up behind me. And I did *not* like anyone coming up behind me, though that's another story. Listening to someone read a book didn't drown out other sounds.

So I ran, and I listened, and I'll be honest: I enjoyed myself. The book was interesting, and the guy reading it did different voices for the different characters. The main characters had just fallen through the eighteenth hole on a minigolf course into another world when I got home, so I passed right by my house and kept going.

I turned around as it started to get dark, but I listened to the book running to and from school every day until it ended. Then I went back for the next audiobook in the series.

As for the librarian, she smiled smugly whenever she saw me in the audiobook section. Then she retreated to her remote lair to weave herself another nubbly cloak or brew some more psychic bookmark tea.

And if she recognized herself in *Gerald in the Grotto of the Gargoyles,* she never said a word about it to anyone, as far as I know.

59

GERALD IN THE WARLOCK'S WEIR was more than a hundred pages long when I saw it next. It was nowhere near done, but it was already longer than *Gerald Visits Grampa*. I didn't read the whole thing again; I just read the new part. Which was a lot.

I don't know how she'd had the time, but Caroline had clearly been reading my (okay, the librarian's) recommendations as she was writing. Even though *Gerald in the Warlock's Weir* wasn't a copy of any of those books, it had a family resemblance, as my grandma Sally would say. It was exciting, and it had some funny parts, and my leg only got twitchy a couple times as I read.

Now I actually got to do what Caroline had offered me ten dollars to do in the first place: take the Red Pen of Boring-Part Detection and point out where I thought things slowed down. There weren't a lot of boring parts, but there were a few, and you will be happy to know that none of them ended up in the finished book. Which means that if you read it and thought there were boring parts in it, you and I will have to disagree on what constitutes a boring part.

Caroline had also done a good job with the flashbacks of

Gerald and Grampa. Almost all of my Nate stuff had gone in, which in my opinion is what makes Grampa such a believable character.

Then I got to the stretch of the book known as the trials. This was where Gerald had to overcome a bunch of dangerous situations before he could get to the warlock's domain and start really hunting for Grampa. Snarko and the Daredevil helped a lot, but it was up to Gerald in the end—he was the hero, after all.

Unfortunately, Caroline had left little notes for me in the margins of this section. Notes like "I need more detail about what it would feel like to run through a Forest of Flaming Ferns" and "How long do you think Gerald can swim in the Frozen Fjord?" and "Let's see what your amazing imagination can do with Gerald's encounter with the Glass Gremlin!" And if that last one sounds somehow less harmful than the others, keep in mind that the gremlin was all jagged edges and slappy attitude—not a good combination.

60

I WAS CONFIDENT THAT MY EXPERIENCE in the stream would do for sensory details about the Frozen Fjord. Besides, it was getting warmer every day, so I wasn't going for a swim under ice anytime soon. And we totally skipped the Flaming Ferns—even Marta wasn't a pyromaniac.

We moved on to what I thought would be the easiest trial: Gerald's journey through the Vale of Violent Violets. If you don't remember them, they look like violets, but they're mean little buggers who stab the ankles of anyone who tries to walk through their vale. With spears.

Marta borrowed a bunch of her parents' plastic appetizer spears for our simulation. They were shaped like tiny weapons with actual points—perfect for a Violent Violet attack. Her arm was back in a sling, since she'd reinjured it trying to prove to her mother how fine it was.

She lay in wait for me in the long grass behind Javier's compost bin, with a fistful of spears. I was supposed to walk unknowingly (at first, anyway, until the attack started) into the violet patch and then get stabbed repeatedly.

Javier smiled in anticipation as he got ready to film the

mayhem. I started walking and Marta started stabbing, but it was clear right away that Javier was disappointed in the level of mayhem.

"You've got to stab him harder than that," he said to Marta after our first attempt. "He barely flinched."

"He's wearing socks," said Marta. "He's protected. And he's walking too fast. Slow down, Alex, and let me spear you good."

"Gerald isn't supposed to be helping the violets out with the stabbing," I said. But it was true that I'd gotten by Marta without feeling much pain. She hadn't even broken the skin.

"Do you want me to take off my socks?" I said. "Maybe Gerald can be wearing sandals."

"Gerald is *not* wearing sandals," said Javier. "He's the hero. He's got to have some dignity."

"Your dad wears sandals," I pointed out.

"Exactly," said Javier.

"My dad wears woolly socks with sandals," said Marta.

All three of us shuddered.

"The problem is that the violets are supposed to be attacking Gerald from all sides," I said. "He can't just step away from them."

"So stand still while I stab you some more," said Marta.

"That's not realistic," I said. "No one's going to stand there and let a bunch of crushable flowers stab him if there's another option."

"I have an idea," said Javier.

And he ran into the house before Marta or I could ask what it was.

61

JAVIER WAS BACK MOMENTS LATER WITH his little sisters, Irene and Emilia, in tow. They did not look happy.

"It's only going to take a few minutes," said Javier to the girls. "All you have to do is get down on the grass—see where Marta is?—and poke Alex with little spears as he walks by. Okay? You like hurting Alex, don't you?"

They did. Irene was nine and Emilia was five, and they didn't agree on much. But they did agree that Alex in pain was good fun. They'd both been there the time I fell off the pogo stick, and I don't think I'd ever seen them laugh harder. Irene was a shin kicker, and Emilia was a biter. I generally steered clear of them.

Javier gave each of them two spears, one for each hand, and positioned them opposite Marta, a few feet apart. "All set?" he asked them. They nodded. "And, action!"

This time through was much more painful. First, Irene stabbed well above sock height. She was obviously going for what she knew were my vulnerable shins. Second, Emilia grabbed my ankle as I went by and started stabbing me in the back when I fell. Then, before I had a chance to get up, Irene and Marta were on me as well, stabbing pretty much everywhere except my face, which I covered with my hands.

All three girls were shrieking like maniacs, and I was yelling at them to stop, when Javier called, "Cut!"

Irene and Emilia took this the wrong way and started sawing at me with the spears until Javier pulled them off. This took longer than it should have because he was laughing so hard.

I thought he was going to tell his sisters off for going overboard and make us try it again, but he said, "Great job, everyone. I think we've got what we need here."

"What *I* need here is about a hundred Band-Aids," I said. "What was that, anyway?"

"You're not even bleeding," said Marta.

"Can we do it again?" asked Irene. "We'll stab harder."

Emilia nodded eagerly. "Much harder."

So that's how Gerald ended up caught in a vine snare and falling in the Vale of the Violent Violets, almost losing an eye in addition to all the ankle-level stab wounds. Caroline, who seemed to be getting as bloodthirsty as Javier's sisters, loved the whole scene when she'd put in my details.

"There's something about those delicate little flowers just going nuts on Gerald like that," she told me when she'd finished.

"There sure is," I said.

62

"**THE GHOST IS BORED,**" **MARTA ANNOUNCED** a few days later at lunch.

I had just finished describing my trip to the doctor, the result of my mother seeing all the red poke marks on my arms and legs and assuming I'd been rolling around in poison ivy. The doctor was mystified, but I was caked with calamine lotion anyway.

"What are you talking about?" said Javier to Marta. "What ghost?"

"What do you mean, what ghost?" said Marta. "There's only one ghost I know of. The Ghost of the Old Weintraub Place."

"Don't tell me you're calling it that now too," said Javier. "It's just someone's house. There are no capital letters."

"How do you know I was using capital letters?"

"I can tell."

"No, you can't. Anyway, everybody calls it that."

Javier groaned into his olive-free Greek salad.

"How do you know the ghost is bored?" I asked Marta.

"Oh, I go over there a couple times a week," she said, popping one of Javier's rejected olives into her mouth.

"What? You can't do that! You don't even have a key. Do you?" I asked. It occurred to me that I hadn't been keeping very good track of the Weintraub key.

"No," she said. "But the lock on the back door doesn't work properly, so I can get in anytime I want. You just have to push a little. Apply some pressure."

All I could say at this point was "Why?"

"I think of it as ghost sitting," said Marta. "You know, like pet sitting?"

"Except ghosts don't need sitting," I said. "Ghosts are pretty independent."

"I figure it might like company," said Marta. "Also, I left my Spanish homework once, to see if it would take the bait."

"Did it?" asked Javier, his fork paused on the way to his mouth.

"Nope. Maybe it doesn't know Spanish. But it left me a note yesterday."

Javier put his fork down. Maybe he was afraid that whatever came next might make him choke.

Which left me to ask, "What did the note say?"

"Wouldn't you like to know?"

"Yes, we would," I said, even though Javier was looking more nauseated than curious.

Marta sat back in her chair and raised her eyebrows at Javier and me. She was reveling in her moment, and we let her.

"It said, 'How's the book coming along?'"

63

"**THE GHOST IS WONDERING HOW THE** book is coming along?" I asked.

"Yup," said Marta. "Maybe it finished all the books in the basement and needs something new to read."

"Did you answer it?" asked Javier.

"How was I going to do that?" said Marta. "Stand there in the kitchen and yell, 'It's coming along well, thanks'?"

"You could have left a note."

"I want to leave the whole book," said Marta.

"So do it," I said.

"My dad won't let me print out something that long unless it's for school," said Marta. "Can I have your copy, Alex? I'll leave it for a few days—like a library book, you know? And then get it back."

I agreed to lend Marta my copy of the book on the condition that I go with her to the Old Weintraub Place. I didn't like the idea of her hanging around there by herself. And just to be clear—it wasn't because I was worried about anything happening to *her*. I hadn't forgotten her plan to "scare the ghost." Could a ghost die a second time of a heart attack if a crazed girl came at it with a TV antenna? Would it become a double ghost then? A ghost squared? I didn't want to have to worry about that.

Plus, the more reasonable part of my brain recognized that giving a fantasy-reading cleaning person a heart attack was way worse than scaring a ghost to its second death.

So Marta and I met at the Old Weintraub Place that afternoon while Javier was at film club.

First she had to make the rounds of the house, upstairs and down, with her stupid antenna, "checking for vibrations." She was sure she detected something in the upstairs linen closet when her antenna jerked, but I'm equally sure it was because the thing got caught in one of those big sticky cobwebs and she had to yank it out.

Marta insisted on writing a note at the end of the book before we left it on the kitchen table.

It said: "How do you like it so far? Does it need more action? Love, Marta."

64

THE BOOK DID NEED MORE ACTION, it turned out. We learned that when we went back two days later.

"You have Earth, Fire, and Water in your trials so far," said the note in the ghost's neat handwriting. "Which seems to leave out Air. Perhaps Gerald could use a flying potion to get over the Sliding Sands and end up being attacked in midair by Diving Doves."

Good idea, right? Though, side note, if I'd known we could fly over the Sliding Sands, I wouldn't have accidentally touched dried-up cat poo in Alvin's abandoned sandbox during filming the afternoon before. The addition of Diving Doves meant, of course, that some sensory detail about whizzing through the air being dive-bombed by birds was required.

Marta was dying to do this stunt. She was the one who came up with the idea to raise the two swings on Irene and Emilia's swing set as high as we could and use them as a harness. She planned to lie across the swings and sort of swim around up there while I pointed a leaf blower at her face to simulate wind resistance and the girls threw stuffed animals at her to simulate the dove attack.

Fine with me. But on the morning of the stunt that Saturday, Marta showed up with her arm in a cast.

"Sorry," she said, holding it up higher than she probably should have. "The doctor says the elbow is never going to heal unless it's immobilized. She says it's this or she puts me in the hospital in traction. I'd like to see her try," she added menacingly. "I can hold the leaf blower with one hand, though, if I brace it in the garden cart."

Which meant I was the one hoisted up on the swings. Which was way more uncomfortable than I'd imagined when it was Marta who was going to do it. Let's just say there was chafing involved, and I ended up wishing I'd worn long pants.

The next problem came when Javier emerged from the house with his sisters and a laundry basket full of their stuffed animals.

"They're good with throwing things at you," he said to me, "but they're worried about the animals getting dirty. So Emilia's going to throw them, and Irene's going to catch them as they rebound off you."

This went about as well as you would expect. Emilia failed to hit me with even one bunny, and Irene failed to catch any of the first half dozen or so that Emilia threw. Then Fluffy or whoever got some dirt on his tail, and all heck broke loose.

"Keep throwing," Javier yelled at his sisters, panning the camera around the swing set while I dangled there, hair blowing in the smelly wind from the leaf blower and legs turning numb. I'd already given up on the swimming motions with my arms—it was too tiring. They were just dangling.

But the girls didn't want to sacrifice any more of their precious animals, so they started grabbing handfuls of damp leaves from the garden bed and chucking those at me instead. Almost all of their clumps flew apart in midair and missed me, except the one that had a rock inside it—that one hit me square on the shoulder. Then Irene threw an old tennis ball that a dog had no doubt drooled all over, and that hit me in the neck.

Meanwhile, the loose leaves were getting sprayed in my face by the blower, and a fleck of leaf wound up in my eye.

I was the one who yelled "cut" this time.

65

"**WHAT ARE YOU WATCHING?**" **ALVIN ASKED** as he came up silently behind me that evening. "With your remaining eye, I mean."

I'd spent the afternoon in the emergency room, having my eye examined. The leaf speck had gotten embedded and had to be removed with special eyeball tweezers. It was gross, and I was glad I couldn't see it while it was happening.

The doctor with the tweezers distracted me by asking about Alvin. "I haven't seen him in here for a while," he said. "Not since the time he made his own contact lenses."

"He still says they made him see better."

"They were made of plastic wrap, so I don't know how that would be possible."

What with the eye patch and the scabby remains of the spear pokes, I might as well have been wearing a T-shirt that said I'M WEAKENED: PLEASE BEAT ME UP. I dreaded going to school on Monday.

I was watching Javier's footage of the day's flying simulation on my laptop, and it was too late to slam it shut by the time Alvin appeared behind me.

After all that effort on the swings, I still had no idea what it felt like to fly—only how it felt to hang uncomfortably. We ended up using some of that sensory detail toward the end of the book, when Gerald breaks into the warlock's tower by dangling on a rope from a hole in the roof. Caroline really appreciated the stuff about the chafing.

"Is that you?" said Alvin, hovering over my shoulder and breathing onto my neck. "What are you doing on those swings? Is that how you hurt your eye? You told Mom you were raking leaves."

I did not need Alvin telling Mom what had really happened to my eye. That would lead to a lot of questions about my activities and my judgment that I didn't want to be bothered with right now.

I decided to appeal to the scientist in Alvin.

"It was kind of an experiment," I said. "To see how it feels to fly."

Alvin nodded. "A third harness would have been more effective," he said. "It would have equalized your weight. Also, not having Javier's sisters throwing dirt balls at you would have helped."

"I'll remember that next time," I said.

"What was the experiment for?" Alvin asked.

"Just, um, curiosity," I tried.

Alvin treated me to his wide-eyed stare of disbelief. Which is incredibly effective, especially from behind the little glasses. He doesn't give up—doesn't even blink—until he gets the truth. My own eyes (patched and unpatched) started to water almost immediately, and I broke.

"Okay," I said, "but you can't tell Mom or Dad. Or Caroline or Lulu. Or anyone, really."

Alvin turned off the high beams and waited for the truth to come out.

66

WHEN I SENT THE DIVING DOVES idea to Caroline, explaining that she needed Air to balance out Earth, Water, and Fire, she sent me an e-mail full of exclamation points about what a genius I was.

This was worrying, because at some point she was bound to find out that I was not a genius and had no idea why air—I mean, Air—was the balance to the other three elements. (I looked it up recently, and the articles got weird and woo-woo pretty fast, so I gave up. Which is why I'm not even going to try to explain it here.)

Caroline did have an objection, though. She said doves were "symbols of peace" and she didn't want them to attack Gerald. Which is why you don't remember a trial involving doves in *Gerald in the Warlock's Weir*. She changed the Diving Doves to Pelting Pigeons, which maybe you do remember. She rejected my suggested tweak, which was Pooping Pigeons. But come to think of it, I'm glad I never had to try out being splattered with bird poop while dangling from a swing set.

So the book was going well, and my stab wounds and chafing and eye injury cleared up, and summer was visible on the horizon, and things were looking good. Except for one small detail. And its name was Alvin.

Now that he'd gotten a full confession out of me about my stunts for Caroline's book, he wanted to be involved. He kept asking me what the next stunt was and how he could "help."

I was forced to sneak out of the house through the basement to film Gerald's fight with the Mime of the Mines, the last of the official trials. It ended up being pretty silly. Mostly Marta combining her version of mime stuff with her version of karate kicks. One of which connected dangerously close to my groin area. Needless to say, that particular detail never made it to Caroline. Gerald had been through enough by then.

The result was yet another video gem that Javier could blackmail me with for the rest of our lives if he chose. I'd just have to hope he got rich and I didn't.

With that, the trials were done. Gerald located the vortex, and with the help of Snarko and the Daredevil, he began making plans to enter the weir and rescue Grampa.

There was only one major obstacle left before the rescue, an obvious one if you are not a reluctant reader and are familiar with fantasy books. Even I, having read one fantasy and listened to three more, knew enough to realize what was next.

A battle. A big, final battle.

I went into training, lifting my mom's lighter hand weights and even doing a push-up every now and then to prepare myself. But when the latest version of the book arrived in my in-box, I was completely unprepared.

The previous chapter title had been "Battle Beckons," and it had ended with the ominous sentence "Even as the friends spoke, the goblin legions were massing on the Pathless Plains." Good stuff. But the next chapter, the new one, which would have been "The Battle of the Pathless Plains" in a world that made sense, was instead entitled "The Peace of the Pathless Plains."

What? Now was no time for peace to break out! Where was the battle?

67

CAROLINE HAD WIMPED OUT. INSTEAD OF an epic battle, she had the goblin army get lost in a Formless Fog, stumble through the Static Swamp, and end up on the Pathless Plains a sad remnant of its former glory. It was pathetic. The goblins were so demoralized, they surrendered to Gerald immediately and everyone went their separate ways. They might as well have been hugging it out and singing campfire songs by the time the chapter was over.

The goblin army wasn't nearly as demoralized as I was, though. I had bulked up for nothing.

Javier and Marta couldn't believe it when I sent my outraged text. Both of them had been looking forward to this as much as I had.

She can't just skip a battle, Marta said.

She owes us! Javier added.

She owes the reading public too, I put in, although I didn't care about the reading public. They'd get over it. I wouldn't.

The new chapter was as boring as the original *Gerald Visits Grampa*. Even if what came after it was a thrill a minute, the sheer lead weight of "The Peace of the Pathless Plains" was going to pull the rest of the book under. The reading public would be fast asleep before they made it to the dramatic rescue. It was only my hope for at least a fistfight or two that had gotten me through it.

This isn't happening, Marta texted.

Not on our watch, said Javier.

We know what we have to do! Marta went on.

This was all sounding so brave and exciting, I felt like the three of us were marching into battle ourselves. I was energized, ready to act, ready to make this right.

I'll send her an e-mail and tell her she HAS to have a battle! I texted triumphantly.

Six different dud emojis came blasting back at me—and those were from Javier.

Marta went with a simple face-palm.

We film the battle anyway, Javier texted. **And we show her how awesome it is. And then she has to put it in.**

THAT'S HOW IT'S DONE! Marta text-shouted.

68

OUR PLAN WAS TO IGNORE THE peace chapter and work with the information Caroline had provided before her epic cop-out.

It became clear right away that the Battle of the Pathless Plains wasn't something we were going to be able to stage in Javier's yard, with Irene and Emilia standing in for the goblin army, though they were hostile enough. It wasn't some small band of goblins we were dealing with—there were legions of goblins. That's what Caroline had written in the "Battle Beckons" chapter.

I looked up "legions" in the dictionary, and it meant a gigantic number. Plus, the goblins had smoke-snorting lizard things that they rode and other equally strange creatures to back them up. And they were "massing," which wasn't a word you would use to describe Mom's book club gathering in the living room. Massing was serious stuff that only legions could do.

Also, by this time Gerald had gathered an army of his own, though there weren't legions of imps, nightwalkers, and swamp dwellers—maybe a couple hundred (plus the one Daredevil). He had to be outnumbered, or what was heroic about the final battle?

"There's no way we can film a live-action epic battle," said

Javier at lunch. "Even if we got the whole school to help, we don't have enough people."

What he didn't have to add was that the whole school would not help.

"Can't you CGI the battle scenes?" asked Marta.

"We're not making a Hollywood blockbuster here," Javier reminded her. "We're trying to see what the battle would really be like."

"I'm guessing it would be bad," said Marta. "Wouldn't it?" She looked at Javier and me in case one of us was going to disagree.

Which we didn't, because she was right. It would be bad. The whole point of battles is hurting lots of people, which meant that I was unlikely to get through even a very scaled-down version of the Battle of the Pathless Plains without lasting injuries, despite my intensive training.

"So if we can't film it with real people," said Javier, "we need to try something else. But first we need to figure out how the battle happens. Do either of you know anything about battles?"

He knew we didn't.

"It's obvious what we have to do," said Marta after we'd sat there for a while, eating our turkey wraps and wishing as usual that there were chips instead of melon chunks to go with them. "We need to ask the ghostwriter."

"How would the ghostwriter know anything about battles?" I asked Marta. I turned to Javier for backup. "Right? The ghostwriter is a reader, not a warrior."

Javier had taken a bite of his sandwich, and now his face turned bright red. I thought he'd let a tomato chunk get past his inspection until he swallowed and rasped, "How would I know?"

"The ghostwriter *is* a reader," said Marta. "Which is the whole point. It's probably read about tons of battles. And wouldn't it be nice to include the ghost in this important scene? We don't want it feeling left out."

69

So we left the stack of pages, minus the dud peace chapter, in the usual place on the Weintraub kitchen table, along with the usual Post-it asking for help with describing an epic battle, and waited. We decided to give it a few days, since there was a lot of new stuff for the ghost to read.

Meanwhile, Alvin hadn't backed off about "helping" with the book. He'd gotten so annoying, I was starting to research boarding schools for him.

"Don't you have something to read?" I asked one day when he was suddenly blowing hot gusts of Cheeto breath on my neck.

"I'm between books," he said.

He began wandering around my room, lifting things and moving things and generally asking to be grabbed by the throat and tossed like a sock monkey into the hallway.

"Can I help you find something?" I asked as sarcastically as I could.

"No, thanks," he said. "I'm fine."

"Then stop messing with my stuff and get out of here," I said. "I'm busy."

"You're not busy," he said. "You're watching some kid see how long he can balance an orange on his forehead."

"It's homework."

"Watching someone trying to balance fruit on his face will never be homework. Unless it's Abnormal Psychology homework. Is that what it is?"

"Yes," I said, "that's what it is. I'm taking Abnormal Psychology. It's a requirement for living with you."

I thought this was pretty cutting, but Alvin just snorted. Then he said something strange. Something strange that turned out to be true, which made it even stranger, looking back on it.

"I'll be around when you need me," he said. "Which will be soon. But the price will be higher than you think."

70

WE RETURNED TO THE OLD WEINTRAUB PLACE on the third afternoon after we'd left the pages. We'd figured this would be plenty of time for the ghost to outline a detailed battle for us, maybe diagram some weird weapons made of logs and strapped together with vines.

I went directly to the last page while Javier and Marta stood eagerly by. I could see right away that there wasn't enough writing on the blank page to describe an epic battle or even a minor argument.

Instead, we got a lecture.

"There shouldn't be detailed battle scenes in children's books," the ghostwriter wrote. "There shouldn't be such battles in civilized society, for that matter. Take a bird's-eye view of the battle, from overhead, in broad detail. Battles are bad enough without having them shoved in your face."

The ghostwriter must have been channeling Caroline. It would have loved the peace chapter. It probably would have contributed the lyrics to a sappy song for the enemies to sing as they held hands/claws.

"Well, that's no help," said Marta after she'd grabbed the page from me to make sure I hadn't somehow been reading it wrong.

"*Now* the ghost gets squeamish?" I asked. "Not *before* I was hit by dirt balls and ended up looking like a pirate?"

"And not in a cool way," Marta added.

"Maybe if the eye patch had been black, it would have been cooler," I said.

"I don't think so," said Marta. "Hey, maybe the ghost died in a battle and has bad feelings about them. That makes perfect sense!"

Maybe it did, but knowing that didn't help our situation.

Javier was reading the ghost's note over and over as if it contained some important clue to his future happiness. Eventually, he sighed and said, "Maybe the ghost has a point. And maybe Caroline is right. Kids' books aren't supposed to be violent, are they?"

"That's what video games are for," I said.

"We don't need blood spurting all over the place and limbs getting chopped off and heads rolling around," said Marta. I wasn't sure what video games she'd been playing, but I was positive her mother wasn't aware of them. "We need to know where the different groups are positioned," she said, "and what their plans of attack are."

"Right," said Javier. "We need strategy."

"Isn't that what a bird's-eye view is?" I asked.

"A bird's-eye view makes everything look smaller," said Javier. "Right? So we need to think small."

"Crud," I said when we'd thought small for a while.

"What?" asked Marta.

"Alvin," I said.

"What about Alvin?"

"He was right," I said. "I hate it when Alvin's right."

71

YOU PROBABLY DON'T REMEMBER, FROM WAY back in an early chapter, my mentioning that Javier sometimes made stop-action films using Alvin's Lego creatures. He used Alvin's creatures for two reasons. First, Irene and Emilia didn't play with Legos, and Javier's mother had given all of his old ones away. Second, Alvin had not only inherited my old Legos, he'd managed to collect a huge number of his own. Practically legions of them. So whenever we needed creatures for a film, we had to go through Alvin.

And the price was always steep.

Also creative. There was the week I had to pull Alvin to and from school in a wagon every day. Not only was this embarrassing, but Alvin plus wagon was too heavy for me to run or even walk quickly with. Then there was the very hot day I had to follow him around with a fan. Not an electric fan—a cardboard one, on which he had written, "Alex lives to serve Alvin." And there was the time I had to try his experimental "energy drink." That one was easily the worst. Let's just say I had barely enough "energy" to cling to the rim of the toilet for several hours after that.

You probably do remember, since it was only two chapters

ago, Alvin telling me that I would need him soon, and that the price would be higher than I thought. *I* certainly remembered it.

So now, as the three of us were walking toward my house and toward Alvin, crouched atop his Lego hoard, all I could think about was what he was going to make me do if we wanted to borrow most of his Lego creatures and a lot of the Playmobil characters as well. I was hoping that maybe, whatever it was, Marta would take over for me. Her arm was out of its cast and ready for action, and she was too.

"Hey, Marta," I began as we arrived at my front steps. "Since you didn't get to do any of the trial stunts . . ."

"Nope," she said. "No way. Whatever your aunt can come up with for Gerald, I'll do. But your brother—forget it. Too risky."

72

THE THREE OF US MADE OUR way upstairs to Alvin's room like Gerald and Snarko and the Daredevil climbing the Stone Steps of the Monastery of Moss, ready to sacrifice something dear to them in exchange for a Parchment of Purpose from the monks. (That's from late in Book 2, if you haven't gotten that far.)

Alvin was lying on his bed, as usual, with a huge book propped on his stomach. I wondered how he could breathe under there.

"Yes?" he said without taking his eyes off the page.

I puffed out a sigh that had been building up ever since we'd figured out what we needed and from who. I didn't want to start with something polite like "Can you do us a favor?" because then it would seem like a big deal and I'd end up changing his future kids' diapers for life. So I went for a casual, no-big-deal attitude. And can I remind everyone that it *wasn't* a big deal? We were asking to borrow some plastic toys—a big portion of which used to belong to me—and return them unharmed.

"Uh, is it okay if we use some Legos for a film?" I said.

Alvin's hand, which had been inside the Cheetos bag, feeling around for crumbs at the bottom, withdrew slowly. He removed the book from his stomach, carefully bookmarked it, and set it aside. Then he sat up and considered his three supplicants. (I got that word from the Monastery of Moss scene, in case you were wondering.)

"Sure," he said. "That would be acceptable."

"Great!" I said. "We'll help ourselves. Thanks!"

I went over to the shelf where the Lego crates were stored. Part of me was wondering what had come over Alvin to make him so agreeable, but I hoped the book he'd been crushed under was really gripping and he just wanted to get back to it. Another part of me suspected that it wasn't going to be that easy. I decided to grab the crates as quickly as possible and scurry out of his room before he had time to think.

"So, purely out of curiosity," said Alvin, who'd already had plenty of time to think, "what are we talking about in terms of numbers? Half a dozen orcs, maybe a handful of monkeys? That sort of thing?"

I stopped, my hand on a crate, and turned around to look at him.

"What difference does it make?" I asked, and even though I'd tried to sound like I didn't care one way or another, I could hear the tremor in my voice.

Alvin heard it too. If he'd had whiskers, they would have been twitching. He sensed my weakness, he hunkered down, and he prepared to pounce.

73

"**IT LOOKS LIKE YOU'LL BE NEEDING** quite a few Legos," Alvin observed from the comfort of his bed as Javier, Marta, and I moved crates into the hallway. "Do you want some Playmobil too?"

"Sure," I said. "That would be great."

Too easy. Way too easy. I was starting to wish Marta had invented some kind of homemade threat detector that would warn us when Alvin's trap was about to snap closed with me in its pitiless jaws.

"What are you working on that requires so many creatures?" Alvin asked.

"Just a video," said Javier, stepping between me and my brother. "The usual thing."

"This seems like more than the usual thing," said Alvin. "This seems pretty epic if you need most of the Legos and the Playmobil reserves as well."

"Oh, it's broader in scope," said Javier, easily playing Alvin's game, "but basically the usual stop-motion video. We appreciate your letting us use your stuff. I'll put your name in the credits; how would that work for you?"

"That would work fine," said Alvin. He picked up his book. I decided then and there that Javier would negotiate all my future deals with Alvin. Then Alvin added, just offhand, like it was an afterthought, "There's one more thing you can do for me, though."

"And what would that be?" I asked.

Marta grabbed my arm like she was trying to brace me. Or maybe like she was afraid this was one of our last moments together.

"I want to do the next stunt for Caroline's book."

Ha! I thought, without letting any sign of triumph appear on my face. Alvin asssumed he was asking for something huge, something I would never let him do under any other circumstances. But he hadn't read the book—he didn't know that it was almost done, that there were no more trials left.

"You know you can't do that," I said. "It's too dangerous. Mom and Dad would ground me for life if they found out."

Clever, huh? I didn't want to give in immediately—he'd smell a rat if I did.

"Well, then, I guess it's too dangerous for me to let you use my Legos," said Alvin. Which made no sense. Ordinarily, I would have pointed that out, but in this case I didn't need to bother with that useless side trip.

I did my best to look angry and defeated. "All right," I said. "If that's the only way, then I guess we'll let you do the next stunt. But you can't tell anyone, ever. Got it?"

"Got it!" Alvin said happily. "Let me know when the next one comes up."

"We will," I said. "The very next one."

And the three of us escaped downstairs with our plastic loot before he could think of anything involving our firstborn children.

74

WE HAD OUR LEGIONS, AND NOW we needed our Pathless Plains. Which quickly turned into a problem.

I'd pictured filming the battle outdoors, but even with my dad's compulsive mowing, the grass in our yard was taller than most of the creatures.

"What about a golf course?" said Marta. "The grass on golf courses is really short, right?"

"Well, if you want the Battle of the Pathless Plains to involve all the armies getting crushed by giants wearing spiked shoes and carrying metal clubs, then that would work," said Javier.

"Sounds cool to me," said Marta.

It did sound cool, but on the other hand, "We'd get yelled at by golfers," I said. "You know, the ones paying to play golf and not to step on Legos."

"What we need is a really big table indoors," said Javier. "That way we don't have to worry about it getting stepped on or rained on."

"Or interfered with by a squirrel," Marta added.

Javier's dining room table was huge, but it was constantly in use.

"I'd offer our Ping-Pong table," said Marta, "but my dad's train layout is all over it. And I'm not allowed to even breathe within four feet of that. Because of the time I drove the train into my face."

Javier and I nodded. We remembered the stitches. Marta had gone out for Halloween as Frankenstein's monster that year. Javier was Dr. Frankenstein, and I was Igor. We'd done well.

"I feel like I've seen a Ping-Pong table somewhere recently," I said. I tried to remember where I'd been. I pictured the table . . . the little net . . . I pictured . . . chocolate-chip cookies. Big ones. "The senior center," I said when I was done processing. "They have a Ping-Pong table. Next to the yoga room. And I've never seen anyone using it."

"Don't you have to be a senior to hang around in the senior center and use the Ping-Pong table?" asked Javier.

"I'm an honorary senior," I said. Nate had told me that the last time I'd been there.

"You really are old before your time," Marta said to me.

So off we went to the senior center Saturday morning, with our Lego crates in the same wagon I'd once been forced to haul Alvin around in.

75

SATURDAYS AT THE SENIOR CENTER WERE busy, it turned out, and I was worried, when we got inside and saw all the seniors milling around, that the Ping-Pong table would be occupied.

But it wasn't.

Javier insisted we get permission to use the table, but there was no one at the front desk to ask. In fact, I'd never seen anyone at the front desk and was starting to wonder if it was fake. Not the desk, but the idea that someone ever sat there, monitoring the entrance or answering questions or whatever.

We went into the common room and found Nate and his clique at their usual table. They were finishing lunch. Ziti, and it looked really good—the perfect sauce/cheese balance.

"Albert!" said Nate. "And you brought your friend Javier and another one."

"I'm Marta," said Marta. "Nice to meet you." She stuck out her hand, and Nate shook it.

"Nice to meet you too," he said. "That's quite a hairstyle you've got there, young lady."

"You think so?" said Marta, reaching up to smooth her half inch of bangs.

"Sure—it doesn't get in your face that way, does it?"

"Never!"

Javier, meanwhile, was glancing around the room like he was looking for someone. Great-Aunt Rosa, I figured. I'd forgotten that she came here, since I hadn't seen her any of the times I'd visited. Maybe she came at a different time of day. Maybe she was a morning senior-center person.

"We were wondering if we could borrow your Ping-Pong table," I said to Nate.

"Sure," said Nate. "Ping-Pong isn't too popular around here right now. These fads—they come and go."

Seniors had fads too? I thought when you got old, you got set in your ways, but apparently not.

So now we had our legions and our Pathless Plains. All we needed to do was film an epic battle. And we needed to make it so awesome that Caroline would realize how wrong she'd been to avoid it. The lingering problem, which we'd been able to ignore while we were concentrating on getting everything together, was that we still didn't have anything like a battle plan. Caroline and the ghostwriter were the ones who supplied the plots. We were the detail crew. How were three kids who knew nothing about battles supposed to film a mind-blowingly exciting one on a senior-center Ping-Pong table with a bunch of toys?

Nate was eyeing the crates, which we'd put down at our feet. "That's a lot of equipment for Ping-Pong," he said. "You do understand it's not a contact sport, right? You don't need pads and helmets for a game of Ping-Pong. Or are you youngsters playing some extreme form of Ping-Pong nowadays?"

Marta had an expression on her face like extreme-contact Ping-Pong was now on her list of things to try. She opened her mouth to say something bizarre, but I cut her off before she could get it out.

"We're making a film," I said. "A stop-motion film of a big battle. These"—I pointed to the crates—"are our legions."

Nate had an expression on his face like the one I'd just squelched on Marta's. "You're filming a battle? With legions? How do I sign on as an extra?"

76

I'D FORGOTTEN THAT NATE WAS A fan of military history. A big fan, it turned out. As in geek level. When we'd explained that we were filming a battle so my aunt wouldn't wimp out on a crucial scene in her book, he sprang into action like a general taking over an army from, well, three kids with no military knowledge beyond the third Lord of the Rings movie.

"So, these Pathless Plains," he said when I'd told him how the "Battle Beckons" chapter had left things. "Any major features or landmarks? Hills, woods?"

"Well, we know there aren't any paths," I said. "And plains are kind of plain, aren't they?"

"What about the surrounding area?" Nate asked.

I had to think for a minute. Where was Gerald now? "Um, the Featureless Fens? And past them is the Static Swamp."

"Ha!" said Nate. "That's a lot of alliteration."

Javier snickered. Marta and I looked at each other and shrugged.

"But not much help in terms of battle strategy," said Nate.

Marta was putting out the Lego and Playmobil armies,

organized by type. "What do we need for the enemy besides goblins and smoke lizards?" she asked me.

I checked my written list. "Glowbeasts, darkriders, bogbears, and weirwolves," I said.

Nate whistled between his teeth in a way I'd been trying to do for years. "Werewolves? This isn't your garden-variety battle, I take it?"

"Not werewolves," I said. "*Weir*wolves. They're the wolves that guard the Warlock's Weir."

"Gotcha," said Nate. He looked over at the table, where Marta was arranging the legions in clumps, facing off on either side of the Ping-Pong net. He crossed his arms. He walked from one end of the table to the other.

Finally, he spoke. "You need some commanders," he said. "Armies don't fight willy-nilly—they need direction."

Willy-nilly. That was going right into my Grampa file.

Marta dug around in the Playmobil crate and came up with a handful of Santa Clauses from various Advent sets. "Will these do?"

"As long as they stand out," said Nate.

The Santas, in bright red and about a head taller than most of the Lego orcs, monkeys, and other creatures we were using for Caroline's troops, definitely stood out.

"But they all look alike," said Javier. "Shouldn't they be different, so we can tell them apart when the fighting gets intense?"

"The fighting is going to get intense?" said Nate, his eyebrows rising.

"It's an epic battle," said Marta.

"Can I just say that I am having a blast?" said Nate.

77

SO NOW WE HAD FOUR SANTAS, an elephant, a soccer coach, and a bus driver as commanders on the goblin side, and a giraffe, a gorilla, and a lifeguard on Gerald's side. Gerald himself, Snarko, and the Daredevil were two Playmobil dads and an actual devil that must have been part of a Halloween set. It wasn't perfect, and we did keep mixing up who was who among the commanders, but it was good enough.

Nate removed the net from the table, then left for a moment and returned with a pool cue, which he used to push the legions around on the table until he was satisfied with their positions. "What have we got in terms of strategic goals?" he asked.

"Well," I said, "Gerald wants to get to the weir, and the goblins are trying to stop him, so they need to battle and it needs to be really exciting, and then Gerald has to win."

"That sounds simple enough," said Nate. "What about strengths and weaknesses among the armies?"

I started to say I had no idea. But then I thought about it for a moment. "The goblins are disorganized and tend to fight among themselves," I offered.

"And the lizards they ride have weak ankles," said Javier.

"The Daredevil has no weaknesses," put in Marta.

"Okay, that's good to know," said Nate. "And your hero? Gerald? Does he have any experience with commanding an army?"

"Nope," I said. "He's an eleven-year-old kid."

"So only playground brawls," said Nate. "Check."

"But he has gone through a bunch of trials recently," I added. "So he's gotten a lot smarter and better coordinated."

"Smarter than your average goblin?"

"Yeah. The goblins aren't very intelligent. But there are way more of them."

"I can see that," said Nate, as Marta continued to add orcs to the goblin group on the table. "Gerald is outnumbered. Which means he needs to outthink his opponents."

That seemed more than obvious now that we had everyone set out on the Ping-Pong table in proportionate numbers (one Lego creature for ten or so of Caroline's). Gerald was in big trouble—it didn't take a military historian to see that.

Nate stood back from the table. "Gerald has something else on his side, though, right?" he asked after a moment.

All three of us thought he was going to go ahead and tell us what that was, but he didn't, so we were forced to start guessing.

"Time?" suggested Javier.

"Money?" offered Marta, which made no sense. There'd been zero mention of money in the book.

"Friends?" I put in.

"Friends, yes," said Nate. "But I assume the goblins and bugbears—"

"*Bog*bears," I corrected.

"*Bog*bears have some buddies too. No, I'm talking about right. Gerald has right on his side, doesn't he?"

"He does," I said. "Gerald is on the side of good."

"Then he can't lose," said Nate. "We just have to make sure of it."

78

IT TOOK US ALL AFTERNOON SATURDAY and most of Sunday to get maybe three quarters of the way through the Battle of the Pathless Plains. Nate's friends stopped by to see what we were up to and offer suggestions. Ellen's ideas got pretty bloody. We had to keep reminding her about the bird's-eye view. She insisted that limbs would be lopped off in fighting like this, and if you remember the battle chapters in Book 1, you will know that a few of her gory details did find their way in.

At one point, Nate decided we needed army medics to remove the wounded. Marta pulled a bunch of doctors and nurses from the crates. "What do I do with them?" she asked.

"Rosa would know," said Henry, who was watching so closely that he was getting cookie crumbs on the legions. There's a point in the finished film where his big pale face is visible, like a full moon looming hugely over the swamp-dweller brigades.

"That's right," said Nate. "Rosa was an army nurse. Where has she been lately? I haven't seen her for months. She used to be a regular for poker."

"Rosa is Javier's aunt," I said. "She comes here all the time, right?"

Javier shrugged. "I thought she did," he said.

Marta had taken this opportunity to start loading doctors and nurses into ambulances and driving them onto the field of battle.

"Wait, wait, wait," I said. "There are no cars in this world!" I thought for a moment. "Maybe carts. Does Alvin have any carts in there? Wheelbarrows or something?"

Marta heaved an annoyed sigh. "We have a soccer coach commanding the glowbeasts and we can't use ambulances?" But she was chucking them back into the crate as she complained. She dug around for a while but didn't find anything cartlike. Alvin wasn't much of a collector of the farm sets.

"Stretchers," said Nate. "They can run in on foot with stretchers and pull out the injured."

Marta and Henry and I found some cardboard in the craft room and made a bunch of tiny stretchers.

So now we had creature armies using real military strategy, and wounded, and even medics. "This is gonna be amazing!" Marta kept saying. "There's no way Caroline isn't going to love this."

Then Nate suddenly said, "Halt!"

"What?" said Javier. "What's wrong?"

"We've got a problem," said Nate.

"What is it?"

"Gerald is going to lose the battle," said Nate. He walked slowly around the table, viewing the scene from all sides. "I can't see any way around it. There's no way he can win."

"But what about having right on his side?" Marta asked. "Isn't that supposed to help?"

Nate shook his head. "I'm afraid in this case, wrong has the upper hand."

79

WE HAD STOPPED FILMING JUST BEFORE dinnertime Sunday, when most of us had to go home anyway. Javier, Marta, and I hurried over to the senior center after school Monday, hoping that Nate had figured out how Gerald could win the battle.

He was standing by the Ping-Pong table when we got there, holding his pool cue by his side. There were also a bunch of Civil War books on a nearby folding chair.

"Any progress?" I asked.

"Gerald is outnumbered," he said. "And now he's pretty well surrounded too."

It was true. The goblins' forces were spread out around Gerald's much smaller group.

"Can't we just get some of those bad guys to back off?" said Marta. "This is fiction. We can do whatever we want, right?"

"It needs to be realistic, though," I said. "It needs to make sense."

"Albert's right," said Nate. "The goblins can't lose for no good reason. We've established that they aren't terribly bright, but that doesn't matter if you've got the numbers on your side. And they do. Even a bunch of idiots can win a battle if it's a big enough bunch."

"Can't you ask Caroline to get rid of some of the goblins' legions earlier?" Javier said to me. "Couldn't she change the numbers?"

"I feel like that's cheating," I said. "We want to make it as hard as possible for Gerald to win. Otherwise, it's not heroic."

"We're definitely making it hard," said Nate. "Our boy Gerald needs a miracle right about now. Something magical."

The three of us looked at Nate and then at one another. Apparently, we'd failed to mention that Gerald had magic available to him.

"Um," I said, "actually, Gerald's grampa is magic. He's a potion master."

"Well, why didn't you say so?" said Nate. "Let's get Gramps to mix up a big batch of sleeping potion. Send the enemy into dreamland for a while."

"We can't do that," I said. "Gerald's grampa is being held prisoner by an evil warlock in a vortex inside the weir."

Nate shook his head. "I hate it when that happens."

80

HENRY HAD WANDERED IN SOMETIME DURING our conversation. "If you've got a potion master and an evil warlock, you must have other magic people around as well," he said. "Can't you get help from someone else?"

"Most of the other magical characters aren't very friendly," I said, thinking of the Glass Gremlin and the Violent Violets and all the others who'd given Gerald attitude and injuries on the way here.

"What about the Absolute Authority?" said Javier.

My heart sank when he suggested this, which was weird, because we were talking about characters in a book. They didn't exist, and they had no right to be able to give someone a sinking feeling. But the Absolute Authority gave me one anyway.

They were a shadowy group of elders who sort of ruled the world that Gerald had found himself in. They hadn't shown up in person, but they'd been talked about by several characters during the trials, mostly in a way that indicated you really, really didn't want to cheese them off. There'd been threats along the lines of "You'd better get off my lawn, kid, if you don't want me to inform the Authority."

"But no one talks to the Absolute Authority directly," said Marta. "You need a blackraven to do that."

She was right. Only a blackraven could even find the Authority, let alone get a message to them.

"So that's out," I said. And I admit I was relieved not to have to involve the Authority. I like to keep a low profile around authorities, fictional and non-, but that's another story.

"What about the pigeon that Gerald saved with the healing salve?" said Javier. "He could find a blackraven."

"That's right!" said Marta. "Vern owes Gerald a favor. His gang attacked Gerald and then left Vern when he broke his wing. If it weren't for Gerald, Vern would have been a weirwolf's dinner."

"Perfect!" said Nate, who had no idea what we were talking about. "Let's send Vern the pigeon out with a message for a blackraven to take to the Absolute Authority."

Or maybe he did.

"What should the message say?" asked Javier.

"Help!" said Nate. "It should say 'Help!'"

81

SO NOW WE HAD A GOOD idea of how Gerald could win the battle, but we needed information. We didn't understand enough about the Absolute Authority to know how it would help or even *if* it could help. Only one person knew that stuff—or at least could make it up for us—and that was Caroline.

"This is awkward," said Javier. "We were supposed to have this awesome battle all laid out for her, and now . . ."

"Now we need her to finish making it awesome," I said.

"Hey," said Marta. "How many times have we gotten *her* out of a jam?"

"A lot," said Javier. "And Alex has the scars to prove it."

"And the permanent limp," Marta added randomly.

"I don't have a permanent limp."

They were right (except for the thing about the limp). And we were almost there. But we needed Caroline to get us over the finish line.

I sent Caroline a carefully worded text. Working on a possible battle scene, I wrote. In case you decide you want one after all. It's going well, but G is outnumbered.

Can he ask the Absolute Authority for help?

It took about ten minutes for her to respond. I was so nervous about having interfered in her book this way that I was jogging the halls of the senior center. The others sat in the common room and ate cookies until my phone finally pinged.

Am in the area, she texted. Will come by asap.

Uh-oh. I had no idea if she was coming to help or to chew me out for making a battle that she clearly didn't want. Plus, she was going to head to my house, where I wasn't.

Am at the senior center, I wrote. Meet me here? She couldn't yell at me in front of a bunch of seniors, I figured. And if she went at me, I knew Ellen at least would have my back.

On my way was the reply.

I met her on the front steps.

"Do you volunteer here?" she asked as we went inside.

"Not really," I said. "Remember when I was doing research for the Grampa flashbacks?"

She nodded.

"I started hanging out here then. The cookies are really good."

"That's enough of a reason for me," she said. "So, um, what's all this about a battle?"

82

I COULDN'T READ CAROLINE AT ALL. She was wearing a suit, since she'd come from work, which didn't help. I was used to casual Caroline, not business Caroline. She didn't seem angry, but then again, I'd never seen her really angry. Maybe she was a quiet fumer like my dad, instead of a red-faced yeller like her sister.

I took a moment to gather my thoughts, but they were sprinting toward the horizon like Marcello on the loose. "Well," I blurted, "I just thought maybe the whole peace chapter was kind of, um, slowing things down, and that maybe an actual battle would be more exciting. You know? The chapter before made it seem like there was going to be one, and then . . . You don't have to do it, of course. . . ."

Caroline rummaged in her purse for no reason I could see except to avoid eye contact. She pulled out an ancient stick of gum, studied it, and dropped it back inside.

I bounced on my toes, getting ready to break into a run.

Finally, she put her hand on my shoulder and pressed down. I stopped bouncing. "It's okay," she said. "I asked you to tell me when the book is boring, and you're telling me. I appreciate that. I was planning to put in a battle, but I got squeamish. I hate violence, and I don't know anything about military stuff. I guess I wimped out."

I held perfectly still to avoid nodding in agreement. "So, you might want a battle after all?" I asked casually.

"I might. If it's not *too* gory. I'm willing to entertain the possibility, at least." She smiled. I smiled back. "You've never steered me wrong before," she said. "But none of this explains what we're doing at the senior center."

"Follow me."

"Oh my" was all Caroline could manage as she took in the sight of the creature-covered table, and Marta and Javier, and Nate with his pool cue and Ellen with her crochet project and Henry being Henry. Then: "What is all this?"

"This is the Battle of the Pathless Plains," said Marta proudly.

Caroline walked over to the table. She put her purse down on it, scattering a herd of darkriders. She reached for a lock of hair and started twirling it as she studied the layout. "And you guys— you all—set this up?" she asked finally.

"Yup. And Javier's filming it," said Marta.

"To get a bird's-eye view of the whole battle," Javier put in, "figure out the strategy."

Caroline's finger was trapped in her hair at this point. She had to tug to get it out. She looked at me. Was she blown away by all our work? Convinced once and for all that an epic battle was essential to the book?

That wasn't the impression I was getting at all.

Then she said, "Alex, can I speak to you privately for a moment?"

83

IF ANYONE EVER ASKS TO SPEAK to you privately, be aware that they aren't requesting privacy so all their praise won't embarrass you in front of others. That's almost definitely not the reason.

We were in the hall outside the Ping-Pong room. Caroline had shut the door behind us. She was pacing in tight circles like a wonky windup toy, her heels clicking on the linoleum floor. I was beginning to think that I might be seeing what she looked like angry.

She stopped clicking around and stood facing me. "So, I really appreciate all the work you've put in on the book. You know that, right?" she began. "And this battle is incredible, it really is. I am blown away."

I nodded. "But . . . ," I offered. Because I knew there was one.

She gave me a pained smile. "But—I wasn't aware that your friends were involved. It took me by surprise, seeing all those people in there."

I nodded again. In my experience, if someone is chewing you out—and she was, though she was being super polite about it—it's best to let it roll over you. Don't even try to defend yourself until they're done.

"When I gave you the book to read," Caroline said, "I wasn't thinking you would be discussing it with other people."

I felt like my stomach was taking a fast elevator down into my knees. I know that's not anatomically possible—would it divide and each half go to a different knee? But that's the only way to describe that sinking sensation I get when someone is criticizing me and I'm realizing that they're right.

It hadn't occurred to me when I let my friends read the book that Caroline might not want them to. Which is weird, because it *had* occurred to me when Alvin wanted to read it. I guess I just thought of my friends as extensions of me—if I could read something, they could too.

That's what I told Caroline. Pretty much in those exact words.

She sighed when I'd stopped talking. I stared up at her, doing what I hoped was a good imitation of Alvin's puppy eyes, though I wasn't sure it worked without the glasses. She didn't seem to notice.

"I get it," she said at last. "And if you'd asked me if they could read it, I probably would have said yes. After all, the whole reason I want to publish this book is so kids can read it, right?"

"Right," I said. Writing a book that you didn't want anyone to read seemed kind of selfish, actually. Why keep it to yourself when someone else might like it?

"Maybe I don't want anyone—besides you and Lulu, of course,

and my agent—reading it before it's done. Seeing it in its underpants, if you know what I mean."

I pictured her poor not-finished book, shivering and embarrassed in its tighty whities. "I'm sorry," I said. "The seniors haven't read it. Only Javier and Marta." I didn't mention the ghostwriter. How could I? "They both really like it," I added.

Caroline clasped her hands like a little kid getting a surprise gift. She cocked her head. "They do?" she said. "They said that?"

"Yup. They said it."

Caroline's face was twitching. It took me a moment to understand that she was doing the thing where you try not to smile but you can't help it, and the trying not to only makes the resulting smile even bigger. Then she put her arm around me and squeezed me so hard, I let out a little cough.

84

BACK INSIDE THE PING–PONG ROOM, AFTER the formal introductions, Caroline stalked around the table, surveying the battle scene.

"So you're the Absolute Authority," said Nate, backing out of her way. "Come to save the day."

Caroline laughed. "No, no," she said. "I am in no way the Authority. I am just the lowly author, and I'm barely in control of this situation. My characters are constantly surprising me. Kind of like my nephew."

"Albert is a great kid," said Nate, poking me in the ribs with the pool cue.

Caroline laughed again. "No argument there." She halted near the middle of the table, where Gerald's army was being clobbered in stop-motion. "I see the problem here," she said. "And there's no way out?"

"No natural way," said Nate. "They're simply outnumbered."

"Well then, something *un*natural is required," said Caroline. "But Gerald can't contact the Absolute Authority himself. That's already been established."

"We were thinking that Vern could get a message to a black-raven," said Javier.

"He could indeed," said Caroline. "That's an excellent idea. Vern owes Gerald his life. And that way his kindness toward Vern leads directly to Gerald's victory. I love that!"

"Plus, Gerald doesn't have to do the asking himself," I said. "So he's still the hero."

"Gerald would be a hero even if he did ask for help," said Caroline. "Even heroes need to ask for help sometimes." She pulled her purse off the table and set the scattered darkriders back on their feet. Or hooves. I was pretty sure they had hooves. "But it makes sense for Vern to take the initiative. He can fly, so he can see from above what's going on, how desperate the situation is."

"He's got an actual bird's-eye view," said Javier.

"Exactly." Caroline studied the ceiling and tapped her chin with a shiny blue fingernail for a while. "So Vern will go for help. . . ." She fished around in her purse and, for the first time ever, came up empty. "Does anyone have a sheet of paper? And some tape?" she asked.

Ellen got them from the craft room.

Caroline rolled and taped until she had an object that looked like a snow cone without the flavored ice in it. "And he will come back with this." She held it out to me, and I took it.

"What is it?" I asked. Origami was not one of my aunt's skills.

"It's a sigh cone," she said. "Get it? S-i-g-h c-o-n-e."

"Not cyclone?"

"Nope, but close. Go ahead, sigh into it."

85

I SIGHED INTO THE SIGH CONE. Nothing magical happened, in case you were wondering. Some warm breath came out the other end. That was it.

"If this were a real sigh cone, and you were Gerald," said Caroline, "you would have blown the wall over there way past the parking lot. And us with it."

"Cool," said Marta. "Can I try it?"

"It doesn't really do anything," I told her.

"I'll be the judge of that." Marta didn't sigh into it—she blew directly at my face.

I got a big faceful of Marta's cookie breath, but I did not crash through the side of the building, leaving an Alex-shaped hole in the bricks.

And yes, Marta did seem disappointed.

"You can't blow into a sigh cone," said Caroline. "It has to be a sigh. Of genuine distress. The more distressed you are, the bigger the wind that comes out of it."

"You just came up with all that?" I asked.

Caroline shrugged.

"Gerald's going to blow those goblin legions to kingdom come!" said Nate happily.

"Exactly!" said Caroline.

Kingdom come, I was thinking. *Good one.*

Caroline raised an eyebrow at me and nodded ever so slightly. I knew she was thinking the same thing.

"So what are those little cardboard strips?" Caroline asked, pointing at the table.

"Stretchers," I said. "For the wounded. The medics run in and take out anyone who's hurt." I demonstrated.

"We're seeing a lot of limb amputations," said Ellen without looking up from the tiny mint-green mittens she was crocheting. "A few heads as well, naturally. And a large number of stab wounds."

"Yikes," said Caroline. She turned to Javier. "So you've recorded all the action so far? And I'll be able to write the battle based on your video?"

He nodded.

Caroline made a circuit around the table. The rest of us watched.

"I'm sold," she said at last. "This book needed an epic battle and now it will have one. Thank you all so much for doing this. I am astounded. Just . . . astounded."

Marta dived in for a hug that looked more like a football tackle. "You won't regret this," she kept saying.

"I'm sure I won't," said Caroline when she was free of Marta's grasp. "But let's stop the mayhem, shall we? Alex, you can do the honors. But since this isn't a real sigh cone, you're going to have to do more than sigh."

"Got it."

I took the cone and got as close to Gerald as I could. And then I blew those goblins to kingdom come.

86

I DIDN'T REALLY BLOW ANYTHING TO kingdom come. I blew some Legos and Playmobil creatures a few inches across the table, and that was only the smaller ones. I puffed until I felt dizzy, then Marta took over. When she got winded, Nate used the pool cue to push whole platoons away from Gerald, which was a lot more efficient.

Eventually, we managed to blow and sweep the opposing armies off the sides of the table, and victory was declared. Javier stopped recording, and everyone cheered.

Nate put the pool cue away and the net back on the Ping-Pong table as Marta, Javier, and I returned the armies to their crates. And if you're thinking Alvin didn't have them organized in very specific ways that we had to carefully re-create, then you haven't been paying attention to my nonexaggerated descriptions of my brother. Marta and Javier argued throughout the process about correct placement, and I kept having to set them straight about Alvin's preferences.

Nate told Caroline to come back any time she needed help with military strategy, and Ellen offered consultations on spear and sword wounds as well. The Rotten Rebellion and Hovering

Hospital chapters in Book 2 are proof that Caroline took them up on their offers.

And Book 1's full moon rising over the Pathless Plains, revealing the trouble Gerald's forces are in right before Vern takes off to find a blackraven? That's based on Henry's face looming over the Ping-Pong table, which Caroline noticed when she watched the video and thought was hilarious.

Caroline drove Marta, Javier, me, and the crates home. She dropped Marta off first, then Javier.

As soon as we were alone in the car, she said to me: "Those two are Snarko and the Daredevil, aren't they?"

I had no idea what to say. I mean, of course they were, but was I supposed to confirm it?

"You don't have to say anything," said Caroline after I'd fiddled with my seat-belt strap for a while. "Your adorable little uncomfortable face tells me everything." She drove on for a while, then added: "They do know, right?"

I nodded, even though she was looking straight ahead and wouldn't see it.

"And they don't mind?"

"No," I said. "They're flattered. Although . . ."

"Although what?" said Caroline.

"Let's say the book gets made into a movie," I began.

"Yeah, right," said Caroline, snorting in an un-grown-up way that made me like her even more than I already did. "Let's say that, just for kicks."

"They'd probably have strong opinions about who plays them."

87

IT WAS GETTING DOWN TO THE last days of school, when no one's head was in the game anymore but we were still going through the motions. Something to do with the legally required number of school days per year, blah blah blah. Even the teachers were phoning it in.

"So when is the book going to be finished?" Marta asked at one of the last lunch periods of the year.

The cafeteria was trying to off-load the leftovers before shutting down for the summer, and some mutant mishmashes were being served. Today we were eating what appeared to be Szechuan noodles with chopped-up chicken nuggets. Some halved grapes floated around in there as well.

"Yeah," said Javier, removing the grape bits from his noodles one by one. "The rest of it went so fast. Shouldn't it be done by now? I want to take it on vacation."

Javier's family always left for the beach as soon as school ended, so time was running out.

"I don't know," I said. "Maybe writing the ending is harder than the rest."

For all I knew that was usually true, but it wasn't in Caroline's case. The book was done. It was sitting on my desk, waiting for me to comment on the last chapters. It had been there for days. I just couldn't bring myself to read it.

A few weeks after we'd finished filming the battle, I arrived home to find Caroline in the kitchen with my mother.

"Alex," she said when I came in to get a glass of water. "I've been waiting for you."

"Okay," I said. "Why?"

"I'm almost done with the book," she said.

She didn't seem as excited as she should have been, in my opinion. I sometimes danced an actual jig when I finished a five-page report, and she was about to finish a three-hundred-and-something-page book.

"That's great," I said.

"I know," she said. "It's really great." She smoothed her hair out of her face even though it wasn't in it. "Can we talk alone?"

"Sure," I said, and headed out, leaving her and my mom to talk about whatever she had on her mind.

"No, Alex, wait," Caroline said. "I meant with you. Can you and I talk?"

I looked at my mom, who shrugged and stood up. "I've got some paperwork I should attend to," she said.

"I have something I need to tell you, and it's hard," said Caroline when Mom was gone.

Oh no. She was going back to *Gerald Visits Grampa* again, wasn't she? The battle had been too violent for her after all.

"What is it?" I asked, bracing myself for zucchini and wondering if the book was far enough along that Javier, Marta, and I could finish it ourselves. Maybe with some help from Nate and Ellen. And the ghostwriter—the ghostwriter could finish it up. . . .

"I'm almost done with the book, as I said," Caroline told me. "And I've had to make a tough decision."

I was really hoping she was being overdramatic and that this had something to do with changing fonts. Although I preferred Times New Roman.

"What is it?" I asked again.

Why didn't she spit it out instead of tormenting me like this? Just because she was a writer didn't mean she could annoy her relatives with cliff-hangers any time she wanted.

She was full-on braiding her hair. A bad sign.

"Was it the battle?" I suggested. "Too violent? 'Cause we can tone it down. I think Ellen got carried away with—"

It looked like Caroline was going for Princess Leia buns at this point, but she let go of her tangle of hair and heaved a big sigh and said, "I have to kill Grampa."

88

"WHAT?" WAS ALL I COULD MANAGE.

Caroline blinked and looked upward, as if doing that would hold in any tears that might have been developing. It wouldn't. We all know this.

"I don't see any way around it," she said. "I really think I'm going to have to kill Grampa. Nothing else makes emotional sense."

I had no idea what "emotional sense" was and I didn't care. "You can't kill Grampa!" I said. "Gerald has to rescue him. If Gerald doesn't rescue him, none of it was worth doing, and he can't rescue him if he's dead."

I sat back, resting my case. She couldn't argue with this logic.

"Gerald already rescued Grampa from the vortex," she assured me. "That part is done. The quest has been fulfilled. But now that it's been fulfilled, Grampa has to sacrifice himself for Gerald so Gerald can take over as potion master. Gerald has to stay in the alternate world and lead the rebuilding after the warlock's defeat. That's the whole premise of Book Two. And he can't do that with Grampa hanging around."

Book 2? Where did Book 2 come from? She wasn't even all the way done with Book 1 yet, and now she was on to Book 2?

Caroline was sniffling and rooting around in her purse for a tissue. She found a linty one at the bottom. She was so much like my mom, who had a whole geological layer of linty tissues in the depths of her purse. I hoped people didn't think Alvin and I were as alike as Caroline and Mom were.

Caroline dabbed at her nose. "You know," she said, "the whole reason I started writing *Gerald Visits Grampa* was because I missed Dad. Lulu and I were just beginning to think about having a baby, and I was wishing he could have been around for it. I wanted to write a book about a kid and a grandfather. For him."

She was outright crying now, which was making me want to cry too. Marta was a domino puker, and it turned out I was a domino crier.

"I'm sorry," I said, wondering if she had another linty tissue in there.

Caroline looked at me with wet eyes. "Sorry about what?" she said. "None of this is your fault."

"Yes, it is," I said. "It's totally my fault. You wrote a nice book about a kid and a grandfather, where the grandfather lived happily ever after with his blue-ribbon zucchini, and I came along and made it into something different, and now Grampa's going to die. I shouldn't have butted in."

Caroline laughed a big teary, snotty laugh, which was both a relief and gross. "My nice book about a kid and his grandfather would be in a drawer somewhere right now if you hadn't butted in," she said. "That book was going nowhere." She blew her nose, thankfully. "And it's still a book about a kid and a grandfather. At its heart, that's what it is. I wish it could have a totally happy ending. But sometimes you can't get what you want, right?"

Wrong! If there was ever a time you *could* get what you wanted, wasn't it in a book you yourself were writing? If you could invent Violent Violets and sigh cones, couldn't you write your way out of a needless death?

"Let me think about it, okay?" I said. "Maybe I can think of a way to make it work where Grampa doesn't have to die. Can I try?"

Caroline grabbed both my hands across the table. Which I didn't love, especially because her damp tissue was balled up in her hand. But I allowed it.

"Of course," she said. "If anyone can come up with an alternative, you can. But I'm going to keep going in the meantime. I want to get this book done before the baby comes. Which is soon."

I nodded. "I'll let you know if I come up with something," I said.

I knew full well I wasn't going to be able to think of anything that made "emotional sense." But I knew someone who might. After all, if anyone could bring Grampa back from the dead, wasn't it a ghost?

89

I DIDN'T WASTE ANY TIME. I went up to my room and ripped a piece of paper out of my history notebook, which had plenty of blanks left in it. I folded it up and put it in my day pack, and then I ran to the Old Weintraub Place.

It was spookier coming here by myself, I realized when I'd gotten inside. I thought about going over to get Javier, but I didn't trust myself not to choke up when I tried to explain the whole Grampa situation to him. This was best handled alone—and quickly.

I hurried through the house, hoping the centipede family and the ghost were outdoors enjoying some fresh air.

I sat down at the kitchen table and wrote a long note for the ghost. I didn't have any more book for it to read, so I explained the situation as best I could. I even used the term "emotional sense," though I'm not sure I used it one hundred percent correctly. At the end of the explanation, I wrote:

"Is there any way Grampa can sacrifice himself for Gerald and get out of the picture without dying?"

I didn't add, *Both my grampas are dead, and I don't want to lose this one too.* But I was thinking about that as I ran home. Gerald's grampa was a great guy, at least according to Caroline's flashbacks. I didn't want him to die. And there was a lot of Nate in him. Stuff I'd suggested myself. Now I felt like I'd put Nate in danger somehow, which was ridiculous, but there you go.

I went back to the Old Weintraub Place the next afternoon and the next, hoping the ghost had come up with a way to save Grampa. But the paper was just as I'd left it both times. On the third day with no response, I gave up and took the note home. I was afraid Marta would drop by and see it, and then I'd have to explain not only why I didn't want Grampa to die, but also why I hadn't involved her and Javier in this.

And then I got the dreaded e-mail from Caroline:

"DONE!!!!" was all it said. But it was enough.

I printed out the end of the book and added it to the stack on my desk without looking at any of the words. And I left it there. I didn't even want to touch it. I felt like it would give me a bad shock or burn me if I did. This was way worse than being a reluctant reader. Now I was a terrified one.

90

WHICH BRINGS ME BACK TO LUNCH and Szechuan-noodle-chicken-nugget-grape casserole (not recommended, by the way—no amount of salt could have saved it). We'd moved on to dessert, which was date bars, probably frozen since the first time they were offered and no one wanted them, back in the fall.

Javier had finished pulling the date bits out of his bar and was now working on the walnuts. Soon he was left with a pile of freezer-burned rubble that he had no intention of eating.

"Send the ending of the book as soon as it's done," he said to me. "I'm not allowed electronics at the beach, so I need time to print it out before we leave."

"You can't rush these things," I said, which was true, but not in the way they probably thought I meant it.

"Yesh, you can," said Marta, chewing on Javier's rubble. "Want me to call 'er up? I'll call 'er up and tell 'er to get a move on."

"You can't threaten someone into finishing a book," said Javier.

"Of course I can," said Marta with a grim determination that made me kind of fear for my aunt.

"What are you going to do?" asked Javier. "Poke her with an old TV antenna?"

"I'll do what I have to do," Marta said. "Plus, we need to bring the ghost a copy. It deserves to know how the book ends."

"You're not still going over there?" said Javier.

"Not much lately," Marta admitted. "I've been busy rehabbing the elbow."

"Is that how you got that giant scrape on it?"

"Dud."

I let them argue while I considered my options. Marta was right. The ghost, not to mention Javier and Marta, deserved to know how the book ended. None of them would mind Grampa's death as much as I did. They didn't have all my grandfather baggage. It probably *would* make emotional sense to them. I had to send the ending to Javier and Marta. That much was clear.

And if I really didn't want to read the Grampa-dying part, I could ask them where it was and skip it, right? I happen to know that my dad used to skip parts of books he read to me when I was little. He confessed recently that he basically rewrote the ending to one of my favorite books while he was reading it to me because the kid in it found out the tooth fairy was his parents, and he didn't think I was ready for that.

If I could isolate the bad part of the book the way Javier did unwanted lunch ingredients, I could read around it. At least then I'd know how the story ended and be able to fix any last boring parts.

My other option, of course, was to just suck it up and read the whole ending.

91

AS I RAN HOME FROM SCHOOL that day, burping up an unpleasant combination of lunch flavors, I thought hard about my options. And I decided that I had to trust Caroline. I had to trust that even if she had written something that would make me sad, she was a good enough writer to make it worth reading anyway.

So when I got home, I sat down at my desk and opened the stack of pages to the new section. Which was when I understood how much I had left to go. I put the stack aside and opened my laptop. I figured I should send the ending to Javier and Marta first, since reading it myself was going to take some time. I gave them strict instructions not to tell me anything about the ending until I had finished. "NO SPOILERS!" I wrote. "NO MATTER WHAT."

Then, being totally honest here, since the laptop was open anyway, I spent some time on the Internet. The kid who balanced fruit on his face had moved on to balancing his face on fruit, which kept me busy for a while.

Then I took a deep breath, gritted my teeth, and started in on the book. I read the battle chapters, which were only sort of new to me, since I knew how it all went down. And I have to say, modesty aside, that the battle made the book way more exciting. Then I read about Gerald and Snarko and the Daredevil finding the weir and figuring out a strategy for getting Grampa out of the vortex.

And then it was time for dinner.

After dinner I went back to the book, bracing myself once again. But Grampa wasn't in the next chapter at all. It was called "The Feast of the Forest," and it was about this big dinner Gerald had with all his allies and buddies in the woods before he attempted to rescue Grampa. It was a funny chapter, with lots of weird guests and weirder food, but Caroline had made some obvious mistakes with the seating arrangements.

I got out my Red Pen of Reseating and drew up a diagram to make sure that no one with spikes was seated too close to someone who was blob based. And that those with tentacles had enough elbow room. And I had to rewrite the bit where someone with no limbs was using a knife and fork. Obviously, Caroline had been rushing when she put that in.

Then I decided I should try to cook some of the dishes she was describing. Just to make sure they worked. It was the same as trying the stunts, only a lot easier.

The tartberry tea was quite good (I substituted raspberries, since tartberries are fictional as far as I know). The butter buns were a little on the dry side, but that was my fault for leaving them in the oven too long. The swamp stew, on the other hand, was awful. Even my dad wouldn't take another bite, and we called him the human garbage disposal, with good reason.

So it took me a few days to get through the Feast of the Forest. Which, yes, was mainly about stalling and not much about recipe accuracy. But if Caroline wanted things to make emotional sense, shouldn't they also make food sense? There was no way even a bunch of backwoods swamp dwellers were going to serve that rancid stew at a feast and get away with it.

The next chapter was called "River Rescue," and here, at long last, Gerald and Snarko and the Daredevil sneaked into the weir and tricked the warlock and finally, finally rescued Grampa. Who was in good spirits, considering. The reunion was touching, and victory felt good after all Gerald's—and my!—trials and struggles. Now they just had to get out of the weir and go home. Right? That's all they had to do.

Unfortunately, the chapter after that was titled "Self-Sacrifice." Crud.

I restacked the pages, squared them neatly, and put them away for another time. School wasn't quite over. There was still homework to do. I don't think I'd ever been more grateful for a bunch of math problems in my life.

92

THE LAST DAY OF SCHOOL CAME and went. Javier left for a week at the beach with his family, and Marta started circus camp, which, she said, was the closest she could get to literary-stunt-double camp. Neither of them had said a word to me about the book's ending.

I usually went to soccer camp during summer days, mainly to keep me out of Mom's hair while she worked, but this summer I was trying something new. I had a job at the senior center, working the front desk. Nate had set it up for me when I'd pointed out that no one was ever at the front desk. He said they had been waiting for the right volunteer, and thanks for stepping up, Albert.

So there I was at the senior center late one afternoon a few days into summer, enjoying a fresh chocolate-chip cookie and getting valuable work experience, when a text arrived from my mother.

Come home now! it said.

She must have known that my reaction would be to break out in a worried sweat, because another text followed right away. Nothing wrong.

I said good-bye to the seniors and rode my bike home.

Mom was already in the car when I got there. "Lu's water broke," she said through the open window. "And Caroline's at work with no car. So I'm taking Lu to the hospital. Dad's on his way home, but it might take him a while. Keep an eye on Alvin until Dad gets here, okay? Thanks!" And she waved and drove away.

Mom was taking Lulu to the hospital because she'd broken her water? Had she dropped a glass of water and cut herself on a shard? Dropped a water bottle on her toe and crushed it? But wouldn't my mom have said she'd broken her toe in that case? I put my bike in the garage and went into the house. Whatever it was, Mom was dealing with it.

I wandered around the house for a while, luxuriating in the feeling of being in charge. Then I went upstairs to see what Alvin was doing.

What he *wasn't* doing was lying on his bed reading. Which seemed strange. Where else would he be? The obvious answer was in my room, messing around in my stuff while he had the chance. I charged in, ready for combat. But he wasn't there either.

I called his name a few times. No answer.

I looked out the window at the backyard, but I didn't expect him to be outdoors, and he wasn't. The basement? The garage?

I checked both before I came to the conclusion I'd been avoiding. Alvin wasn't here.

93

ALVIN NEVER WENT ANYWHERE WHEN HE didn't have to. And he wasn't allowed to wander the neighborhood by himself—he was eight and had a history of getting into trouble in his own room. So where had he gone without permission while Mom was getting ready to drive Lulu to the hospital?

I looked all over the house one more time, because I've been known to panic, thinking that something—like my phone or my backpack or last night's homework—was missing when it wasn't. But my brother was definitely missing.

I checked his room for clues. Maybe one of his experiments required something he'd had to leave the house to get. But there was no sign he'd been working on anything in there. There wasn't even a book on his bed.

Then I checked my room. Maybe he'd broken something and sneaked out of the house to avoid my wrath. But Alvin wasn't afraid enough of my wrath to leave the house. I knew that.

I was getting ready to give up and call Dad, when I saw what I'd been looking for. A clue. A subtle orange clue.

Caroline's book was on my desk. It looked almost exactly the way I'd left it when I stopped reading a few days ago. But not quite. There were two stacks of paper, one large and one small. The small stack had the chapter "Self-Sacrifice" on top, still staring at me threateningly. But there was one difference. The first page of that chapter had orange fingerprints on it. They weren't my fingerprints. I wasn't the one who ate Cheetos compulsively whenever he read anything.

He might as well have left a neon-orange sign that said ALVIN WAS HERE.

Alvin had been reading Caroline's book, and now he was gone.

I sat down hard on the desk chair and thought about what that meant. Then I remembered my promise to him when we'd borrowed his Legos. That he could do the next stunt. I'd thought there were no more stunts, but I didn't know that for sure, because I hadn't finished the book. I flipped to the last page. Sure enough: more Cheeto prints. He'd read all the way to the end.

I could only assume that he'd found a stunt in there and seen his opportunity to try it when Mom got the call from Lu.

And the only way I could find out what the stunt was, and have any idea where Alvin might be now, was to read.

94

THE FORMERLY RELUCTANT READER WAS NOW the wincing, cringing, rushing reader as I tore through the chapter I'd been avoiding. Maybe it was like ripping off a bandage and going fast made it easier, but I got through Grampa's death scene without even sniffling.

The warlock caught up with Gerald and Grampa at Grampa's house and basically tossed them into the slipstream, sending them back to their own world. Then he destroyed the slipstream, stranding them there. And funnily enough, the only way they could return to the alternate world was by using a hidden slipstream that Grampa had set up—in a storm drain. So my idea about Gerald the frog falling into a storm drain from way in the beginning got in there after all. Even though I'd never mentioned it to Caroline. Great minds really do think alike.

Gerald and Grampa managed to slide into the storm drain slipstream and get back to the alternate world for one last showdown with the warlock. And Grampa threw himself between Gerald and the warlock when the warlock sent a killing spell Gerald's way, and it hit Grampa instead.

Bad, right? Heroic, but bad. I would definitely have been sad if I'd stopped to think about it. But as soon as I got to the end of the chapter, I realized what Alvin was up to.

I don't know how familiar you are with the storm drains of your neighborhood, but Alvin and I knew the ones around us well. We'd always enjoyed throwing pebbles into them and hearing the pebbles *plop* into the dark water below. Most storm drains are set so close to the curb that there's no way a grandfather or even a boy could slip into one of them. I'm sure that's by design. No one wants people randomly falling into storm drains all over the place.

So on the face of it, Caroline's last stunt was impossible. No storm drain was going to fit Gerald and Grampa. Using it for a slipstream substitute didn't make sense. I knew this, and I'm guessing Alvin knew it too.

Except there was one storm drain that maybe—*maybe*—was big enough. The one by the soccer field between here and Javier's house. The curb was really high there, and the grate was low. There was a sizable gap. And if I had been reading that chapter and wondering if Caroline's idea might actually work, that's where I would have gone to check it out.

I didn't wait around to leave Dad a note or make any other rational decisions about how to proceed. I slammed the front door and started to run.

95

I DON'T USUALLY RUN FOR SPEED. But I made it to the soccer field in what I'm sure was record time, and I was winded when I got within sight of the storm drain. I stopped to catch my breath and scan the area. There wasn't a single person on the field or the jogging track that circled it. The sky was cloudy, and it was starting to rain those big fat warning drops that mean you are about to get drenched.

At first it didn't seem like anyone was hanging around the storm drain, taking measurements or whatever. But that's because I was looking for a person standing by the storm drain. Not sitting on it. Not sort of lying on it. Which was what Alvin was doing. I could see him now that I was focused at curb level. He was lying on the storm-drain grate, and he was waving at me.

I ran over there, ready to let him have it about wandering off and not telling Mom and lying on a filthy grate. After that, I was planning to get into being in my room when I wasn't home, reading a book I had told him not to read, and getting his Cheeto prints all over the place.

But when I got close enough to him to begin the yelling, I

couldn't do it. He was covered with grime, both of his legs were partway down the storm drain, and—most important—he was obviously stuck.

Crud.

"Thank goodness you're here," he said, sitting up as best he could. "I got my legs partly in, but now I can't get them out. See?" He pointed at his legs in case I needed a visual aid. "I'm thinking Grampa is going to have to concoct a slimy substance of some kind. That might enable Gerald to slide in here. Although I'm sure Grampa would never fit. Unless he has super-skinny legs. Does Grampa have super-skinny legs? I don't think that's been mentioned, if so. You didn't happen to bring anything slimy with you? Some butter or olive oil? Or soap. Soap might work as well. Liquid soap would be best."

I stood over him with my hands on my hips. "I ran out of the house to come find you. I didn't stop to bring any soap with me. Although you could use it. Look at you—you're filthy!" And, for the record, I sounded exactly like our mom as I said all this.

Alvin shrugged. "You promised me I could do the next stunt. Remember?"

"Yes, I remember," I said. "But I didn't say anything about doing it alone. Did you see me doing any of the other stunts alone? You didn't. And why is that? Because it's a stupid, danger-ous, dumb, idiotic, stupid thing to do!"

"You said *stupid* twice."

96

I CLENCHED MY FISTS TO KEEP from yanking Alvin out of the storm drain by his ears, leaving his lower legs behind if necessary. I took a calming breath, blew it out, and then crouched to see what I had to do to remove him. Surely it was simply a matter of advanced physics. Too bad we didn't get to advanced physics until high school.

"I think if you turn your legs sideways, then—" I began.

"I already tried that," said Alvin. "I've tried everything. I think we're going to need the Jaws of Life. You know—the tool they use to get people out of crumpled-up cars. I think that's the required implement in this situation."

He looked at me expectantly, like I might have a set of Jaws of Life in my back pocket.

"If I didn't bring any soap, what makes you think—"

"I know you don't have them. Only emergency personnel would. You're going to have to call 911. Do you have your phone with you?"

Of course I had my phone with me. I had my phone with me in the same way I had pants on.

"We are not calling 911," I said. "That's for serious emergencies only. Believe me, I know."

"Maybe we can flag down a police car," Alvin suggested. "But we can't wait too long. It's raining. We're getting wet."

If you're thinking that Alvin was being quite calm during this discussion, especially compared to me, you're right. Alvin had been in tight spots before—figuratively and also literally. You would be amazed at the variety of places he'd gotten his head stuck over the years. He wasn't afraid of much.

There was one thing he was afraid of, though. One thing he truly hated and feared. And unfortunately for us both, that very thing was about to enter the picture.

97

THE SKY HAD GOTTEN DARK, THE rain had gotten heavier, and a strong wind had decided that now was a good time to start blowing the rain sideways across the soccer field.

The rain plastered our hair to our heads and soaked our clothes. Meanwhile, Alvin's storm drain was trying to do its thing but mostly failing. Dirty gutter water ran toward it, but instead of spilling into it, the water and its floating muck swirled around a big clog named Alvin. None of this was great.

Then we heard a loud rumbling noise.

"Was that a truck going by?" asked Alvin nervously. "I think that was a truck going by and hitting a pothole. Or a train? Do trains hit potholes?"

It wasn't a truck or a train hitting a pothole. We both knew that the rumble was thunder. And that thunder would be accompanied by lightning. And that lightning was the one thing Alvin was afraid of.

With good reason. Lightning isn't one of those irrational fears like, say, clowns. There are no red warning bars at the bottom of the TV when clowns are sighted in the area. No one tells you to take shelter immediately when you see a clown on the horizon. Lightning is a totally rational fear. I wasn't a huge fan myself.

"I think it was a truck," I lied. "Just concentrate on getting unstuck, okay? Remember what Dad always says: If you can get it in, you can get it out."

He nodded, but then the sky lit up.

Crud on a cracker.

With that flash of lightning that definitely hadn't come from a truck, Alvin lost his cool immediately and completely.

"Get me out of here. Nooooow!" he wailed, and he started struggling and thrashing and grabbing at me like he was drowning.

"Alvin," I yelled over the thunder that followed the lightning flash, "you need to hold still. I think the rain will help loosen your legs, but you have to turn them to the side, okay? Can you do that?"

He nodded and his wet Gollum hands let go of my forearms.

"Good. Now, first turn your right leg. About ninety degrees." Alvin liked things that could be expressed in degrees. "Got it? Okay. Relax your leg. Let it go limp. I'm going to gently, gently pull ..."

I think I would have had that first leg out if one of those jaggedy lines of lightning that look like Zeus is angry hadn't crackled down the sky at that moment. Alvin and I both yelled at the same time. Then my little brother looked up at me with his huge scared eyes and wailed, "Alex, you need to call 911. *Now!*"

98

I REALLY, REALLY DIDN'T WANT TO call 911. You already know that.

What you don't know is why.

The reason I hated the idea of calling 911 was another story altogether, as I may have mentioned once or twice. A story that had nothing to do with this one.

Except, as Caroline would say, this story doesn't make emotional sense without the other one. Because if you don't know why I hated the idea of calling 911, you're going to be thinking along the lines of: Why is this kid worried about making a simple phone call when his little brother is trapped in a storm drain amid dangerous and terrifying bolts of lightning?

So here's the other story. You forced it out of me.

It happened when I was ten, back when I walked from place to place instead of running. I had just gotten my first cell phone, which was *for emergencies only*, my parents told me again and again. My dad, who has one of those label makers that only crazily organized people use, put a label on it that said FOR EMERGENCIES ONLY.

I was walking home from school when I noticed a car following me slowly. I knew about stranger danger, and a slow-following car was definitely a warning sign.

I started to run, and I kept running until I got to a busy street and had to wait for a walk signal. The car that had been following me passed through the intersection and pulled over to the curb ahead.

I was only ten, remember, so the things I thought and did weren't perfectly logical.

I saw the car pull over, figured some kidnappers were lying in wait for me, and panicked. Instead of turning around or crossing the street, I got out my phone *for emergencies only* and I called 911.

"I think someone's trying to kidnap me," I told the operator.

She said a squad car was right around the corner. What seemed like hours went by, and I was close to wetting my pants with fear that the kidnappers were going to lose patience and jump out of their Kidnapper Car to grab me. But I stayed put, because that's what the 911 lady had told me to do.

Then a police car pulled up. The officers got out and asked if I was the kid who'd called 911. I said I was, and I'm sure I sounded truly scared when I described the Kidnapper Car and its suspicious movements. They were patient and nice to me and said they would check it out.

The officers went over and talked to whoever was in the car. It looked more like a chat than an arrest going down. Then one of them came back to me. And she didn't seem nearly as patient and nice on her return.

"Is your name Alex Harmon?" she asked me.

I said it was.

"And is that your backpack?"

"What?"

"Is that your backpack you're carrying? The one on your back," she clarified when I continued to look baffled.

I took it off and studied it. It wasn't my backpack. It only looked like mine. "Um, no. I guess not."

She stuck out a hand, and I gave her the backpack that didn't belong to me. "Wait here," she said. She took the backpack over to the Kidnapper Car and handed it inside. Then whoever was inside the car handed her a very similar backpack—mine.

99

THE KIDNAPPER CAR BELONGED TO Caleb A.'s mother. Caleb A. had a backpack like mine, which I had taken by accident when I left school. Mrs. A. had been following me slowly because she didn't want to freak me out by yelling at me from her car.

All a big misunderstanding.

Which would have been fine, except that the police officers seemed to think I needed a lecture about identifying one's personal property correctly and differentiating between dangerous cars and classmates' mothers' cars.

I could feel the red heat crawling up my neck and face as they spoke to me in their official voices. I could feel a pit opening up in my stomach. I stared at the real, working guns in holsters on their belts and the handcuffs and all the other equipment they had available. I was terrified they were going to arrest me. By the time they were done talking, I had stopped listening and was almost in tears. I had never felt so guilty in my life—including the time I bit Alvin's neck and made him *bleed* during my vampire phase.

I put my backpack on when they had driven off, and I ran all the way home.

I never told my parents or any of my friends what had happened. I felt too guilty and too stupid and I was afraid I might cry if I tried to talk about it. I worried for weeks that the police were going to call or show up at our house and rat me out to my parents. I was also so jumpy whenever I sensed a car following me that I started running everywhere. No one could sneak up on me if I was already running. And even after I stopped feeling jumpy, I kept running. It felt natural by then, even good. Plus, it was a lot faster than walking.

So that's two backstories for the price of one: the story of why I hated everything to do with 911, and the story of why I ran everywhere. Psychologically complex I was not. Scarred for life, though, was a real possibility.

100

I HOPE MY EARLY EXPERIENCE WITH calling for help explains what I did next. Which was not dial 911 and get professional aid in removing Alvin from the storm drain. I was terrified that if I did, a pair of police officers—maybe even the same ones from before—would arrive with siren wailing and then tell us off for trespassing on a government grate. I pictured them writing down our names, saying, *See you juvenile delinquents in court*, and peeling out toward a real emergency. Maybe chucking a bottle of liquid soap at us if they were feeling generous.

So instead of calling 911, I said to Alvin, "I have an idea. Take your shoes off. Then we can wiggle your legs out without them."

"That won't work," said Alvin. "It's not my feet that are stuck, it's my legs. I think I've had a growth spurt in my legs since I put them in there."

That was ridiculous, of course, but so was my idea about his shoes. Which I persisted with because I was frantic and desperate. "Just do what I say and push them off!"

"I can't," Alvin said. "I'm too stuck to maneuver properly."

I went into angry-Dad mode, quiet and fake calm. I lay down on the grate next to Alvin and reached into the storm drain. My face was down with the swirling muck around Alvin's butt. And also with Alvin's butt. I managed to grab hold of one of his soggy sneakers and yank it off. I brought it out in triumph and set it down by the grate. Then I went back for the next one.

As my arm was groping around in there, Alvin started wiggling, and I heard his other shoe *plop* into the water below.

"There," he said. "I got the second one off. Can we go now?"

But Alvin's wiggling had pulled my dangling arm farther into the drain. My arm was wedged between the grate and the curb along with his legs. I struggled and tugged and twisted, which only skinned my elbow and lodged the arm more firmly.

There were three Harmon limbs hanging above the dark water, and in that situation is there anyone who wouldn't have wondered if there was such a thing as storm-drain sharks? I was about to ask Alvin if sharks were strictly saltwater fish, when he said, "You know those stories about people getting exotic pets like piranhas or maybe alligators and then dumping them in the sewer when they get too big or possibly aggressive, and—"

"Nope," I said.

We sat/lay there getting rained on for a few minutes, thinking our own thoughts. Mine were about storm-drain predators. I'm guessing Alvin's were as well. A car appeared, and we both yelled for help at whoever was driving, but the car only sprayed water over us as it sped by.

"Why would someone just drive past two kids obviously trapped in a storm drain?" I asked Alvin.

He peered out from under my T-shirt, where he was trying to take shelter. "Maybe they thought we were playing here. Maybe they thought we were having fun."

"Do I look like I'm having fun?"

"I mean," said Alvin, "you do look pretty funny. . . ."

101

I COULDN'T HAVE CALLED 911 IF I'd wanted to with my arm stuck in the storm drain. Trying to use my phone in this position guaranteed that the phone would end up in the depths with Alvin's sneaker. Panic was beginning to make a nest for itself in my lower stomach.

It got even worse when I noticed a large rodent scampering toward us.

Maybe storm-drain sharks were impossible, but sewer rats sure weren't. Here was a giant sewer rat in the flesh, and here were two boys blocking the entrance to its home. Although, would a sewer rat live in a storm drain? What was the difference between a sewer and a storm drain, exactly? Where was Javier the walking Wikipedia when I needed him?

"Alvin—" I began quietly, but he cut me off.

"We're saved!" he cried. "Look, Alex! Marcello is coming to rescue us! Yay for brave Marcello!"

The sewer rat was Marcello, and he was barreling toward us, yapping up his own storm. He slowed as he got close. He trotted over to Alvin and started licking any exposed parts he could get his tongue on.

"Marcello," said Alvin, hugging the wet, smelly dog, "we're trapped in here. Go get help, boy!"

Marcello finished coating Alvin with slobber and jammed his nose into my armpit. It was cold and wet, and I jerked my arm reflexively, freeing it from the storm drain. I sat up and rubbed my sore elbow.

"See, Alex?" said Alvin. "He's a rescue dog, aren't you, Marcello! He's our hero. Good, good dog, Marcello! Now, go get help, good boy!"

It's possible that Marcello's yapping was meant as encouragement, or even instructions. But it didn't help. And neither did what Marcello chose to do next. Which was get me back for all the times I'd disrespected him by stepping over him on the sidewalk. All the times I'd ignored his pestering as I ran. All the times I'd called him a little rat-dog to his little rat-face.

He raised a leg and peed down my back as I sat on the sewer grate. Then he yapped a final yap for good measure, picked up Alvin's sneaker, and tore off with it in the direction of home.

102

MAYBE IT WAS ALVIN'S NEWFOUND HOPE that Marcello was headed home to yap out our exact dilemma and location to his owners: "What, Marcello? Our cute neighbor Alvin is stuck in a storm drain over by the soccer field? And he needs liquid soap? On our way!" Or maybe it was the cool rain making his legs smaller and slipperier. We'll never know, but as Alvin watched Marcello "go for help," he calmed down enough to cooperate as I carefully turned his legs to the side and worked them out of the storm drain.

Meanwhile, the lightning flashes and thunderclaps were getting closer together, which meant the storm was getting closer to us. And there we were, out on the edge of a flat field with no shelter in sight. Lightning bait, in other words. Alvin kept trying to cover his ears and eyes at the same time, but the poor kid only had two hands.

I looked around for something, anything, to get inside or under or even near: a shed or an overturned wheelbarrow or a cardboard box. I wasn't feeling picky. But there was nothing.

"I wanna go hooome!" Alvin yelled after a particularly loud boom of thunder.

"Okay, okay," I said. "We're going to have to run for it."

"I can't run without sneakers!"

"Of course you can."

"You need to carry me!"

Crud on a cracker with a side of creamed crud.

"I'll piggyback you, okay?" It wasn't a great plan, and I wasn't going to be able to run very fast with my soaking-wet brother on my back, but this seemed like the only option.

Then I realized that the houses backing up to the far end of the field were on Javier's street. We were closer to Javier's house than we were to our own. Javier would take us in. Javier would give us shelter. We could call Dad from there, and he would come pick us up, and our nightmare would be over.

I had Alvin on my back and was running toward the safety of Javier's house when I remembered that his family was at the beach. There would be no one there to take us in and give us shelter. I kept going in that direction, though, thinking that maybe they'd left the garage open, or if not, we could huddle on the porch. Then I thought of something else.

The Old Weintraub Place. It was even closer than Javier's.

I realized as soon as I'd had that brain wave that not only had I foolishly left home without any liquid soap or Jaws of Life, but I'd also left without the key to the Old Weintraub Place.

My burdened running slowed, then sped up when a pretty much simultaneous flash of lightning and clap of thunder put a new spring in my step. At which point I recalled something

Marta had said about the lock on the back door of the Old Weintraub Place being broken. "You just have to push a little," she'd said.

I could do that.

LOCAL BOY HEROICALLY CARRIES BROTHER THROUGH STORM TO
SAFETY is the headline that never appeared in the town paper.
Because no one saw us as we (well, I) ran across that field like
something was after us. Maybe Zeus, with a big bucket of lightning bolts. No one was stupid enough to be out there except me
and my brother.

At one point, my passenger pulled on my hair like a rein and
called into my ear, "Alex, stop!"

"Ow! No! We're running for our lives here, in case you haven't
noticed!"

"But Marcello. What about Marcello? We won't be there when
he gets back with the team of rescuers."

I pretended I was too busy running to answer, but there was
no way Marcello was dashing back to the storm drain at the head
of a pack of rescuers. If I knew Marcello—and I did—he was at
home now, in his cozy doggy bed in the bay window, happily
chewing Alvin's sneaker to pieces.

I dumped Alvin on the grass when we reached the Weintraub
yard and said, "We're going in here."

"The Old Weintraub Place?" he asked as we went up the back steps. Which proved that Javier was wrong, and everyone did call it that. "We can't go in here. That's trespassing."

"It's taking shelter," I said as I pushed on the door. Which didn't budge. "It's just to get out of the storm. We'll call Dad from here. We won't touch a thing."

I pushed harder, and the door continued not to budge. Had someone fixed it since Marta had been here last? I wasn't sure when that was. It was also possible, though, that Marta's idea of pushing "a little" wasn't the same as mine. I put my shoulder to the door and shoved. Sure enough, it opened, and I stumbled into the dim kitchen. Alvin practically trampled me to get inside. Then he turned and slammed the door shut for good measure.

I grabbed some paper towels from the counter and told him to dry off. Then I went to work on myself.

"You said we wouldn't touch anything," Alvin protested. But he sat down on the floor and started carefully blotting his muddy socks.

I was about to reply with my usual older-brother logic when I saw a piece of paper on the kitchen table. It hadn't been there when I'd picked up my note last time. Maybe it was a message for the cleaning person. If it was, I would add something about needing more paper towels.

But the note wasn't for the cleaning person. It was from the ghost. (Who could have been a cleaning person, if you've been keeping track. Though I don't blame you at all if you've given up on that.) The message was for me. It was about the book, about Grampa's sacrifice. It started out, "Here's an idea that might enable Grampa to make a sacrifice without dying."

I put down my wad of paper towels and picked up the paper. Which was when Alvin said, completely out of the blue, "Are there ghosts in this house?"

"Why would you think there were ghosts in this house?" I asked. I folded the paper and put it in my pocket for later. "Just because it's empty doesn't mean there would be ghosts."

Alvin flinched as thunder rumbled overhead, but it wasn't as loud now. The storm was moving away.

"I heard something," Alvin said. "Like a ghost noise."

"What's a ghost noise?"

"Listen," said Alvin.

We stayed quiet, listening. And then I heard what he'd been hearing. A low moan. Like a ghost noise.

104

IN ALL THE TIMES I HAD been in the Old Weintraub Place, I had never heard an actual moaning-type ghost noise. And neither had Javier or Marta. It was something they would have mentioned.

The fact was, if any of us had ever heard an honest-to-goodness ghost noise here, none of us would ever have come back. We came back because, deep down, we didn't believe there was a ghost haunting this house. I don't think even Marta truly believed it.

But now? I didn't know what that noise was, but it sounded way more ghostly than any noise I'd ever heard in real life.

"The storm's moving away," I said to Alvin. "We should go home. It isn't as dangerous outside now." *As it might be in here* was definitely the unspoken end of that sentence.

"If you can hear thunder, it's still dangerous," said Alvin. "Besides, we need to find out what that noise was."

We really didn't. But as I said, Alvin was only afraid of lightning. So given the choice between lightning outside and ghost noises in, Alvin was going to stay in. And given a mystery, he was going to try to solve it. He stepped toward the basement door. "I think it came from here," he said. And he opened the door.

Alvin opened the door to the place where the scary noises were coming from because he'd never seen a horror movie. I had. (Accidentally, at a sleepover. My parents were not pleased.) I knew that opening the door was the last thing you wanted to do in this situation.

With the door all the way open, we could both clearly hear what came next. Which wasn't a ghost noise. It was a person noise. And the person was saying, very softly but not so softly that we couldn't hear it, "Help. Help me. Please."

Alvin ran down the basement stairs immediately. I followed him into the darkness, wishing that one of us was wearing Marta's flashlight helmet.

Alvin stopped at the bottom of the stairs. "There's someone here," he said quietly, as if he didn't want to disturb whoever it was. "Lying on the floor."

105

IT WAS SO DARK IN THE basement that I had to wait until my eyes adjusted before I could see what Alvin was talking about. When they did, I saw what looked like a heap of laundry on the floor.

"Are you okay?" Alvin asked it.

There was a sigh from the laundry heap. "Obviously not," it said.

And here I have to mention that although Alvin may have been a pitiless negotiator, he had a big heart. He knelt on the floor and reached into the laundry heap and took its hand. "We'll save you," he said.

I went around Alvin to the other side of the person lying on the floor. Which was when I recognized her. "Great-Aunt Rosa!" I said.

"None other," she replied faintly. Her face glowed ghastly white in the dim basement. She was flat on her back. "I fell on the stairs," she said. "I think I broke my hip."

"But what are you doing here?" I asked. Which, looking back on it, wasn't the first thing most rescuers would have asked.

"I came down to get a book," she said.

This response invited a lot of questions. The first one that came to me was:

"Aren't you supposed to be at the beach?"

"I stayed home to have some time to myself. Then Marina decided to stay home too. So I came over here to read in peace." She looked at Alvin when she said, "Big sisters. Am I right?"

Alvin nodded readily. "I've got a big brother. Same thing, though."

Great-Aunt Rosa closed her eyes.

"She needs help," Alvin whispered. Like he was afraid Rosa might find out she needed help if she heard him.

"I know," I said. "I'll go get Marina."

Rosa's eyes opened. "Useless," she managed. "Also . . . at the mall." Her eyes closed again, and she sighed at the uselessness of older siblings everywhere.

"I'll call Dad," I said. "He's probably home by now."

Alvin shook his head. "Dad's an accountant," he said. "She doesn't need her taxes done. She needs an ambulance. You have to call 911."

AUNT ROSA'S EYES WERE CLOSED, BUT Alvin's were wide open and staring at me, begging me to do what needed to be done.

"I have to go upstairs to call," I said. "The reception won't be any good down here." Not exactly a lie, since it might have been true, but it was not my reason for going upstairs.

"Okay," said Alvin. "But hurry!"

In the kitchen, I sat down at the table and got out my phone, which was damp and gave off a whiff of dog pee. I wiped it with a paper towel and immediately called not 911 but Dad. It went to voice mail.

Crud on a cracker topped with crud croutons.

I didn't leave a message for my dad. Where would I even begin? I stared at my phone. I brought up the keypad. My finger hovered over the 9. I put the phone down, my hand trembling.

I needed to call for help. This was an actual emergency. Aunt Rosa was a nurse, and if she said she had a broken hip, she knew what she was talking about.

Then again: What if it was just a sprain? What if the EMTs got here and picked her up and said she'd be fine, and then turned to me and said, *Are* you *the kid who called 911 about this minor injury?*

Then again *again:* What if Rosa was hurt really badly and she was being brave and trying not to scare us? What if she was in big trouble and every second counted?

"Alex!" came Alvin's scared voice from downstairs. "She's all sweaty!"

She wasn't the only one.

It's exciting when you're reading a book and there's danger. Danger makes a book that might otherwise be dull more interesting. That was my theory when I'd started making suggestions about Caroline's book. I'd wanted Gerald swept down a storm drain way back when he was still a frog. I'd wanted to add danger from the very beginning. I'd made her add a whole battle because I thought it would be thrilling.

But I'm here to tell you that real-life danger isn't exciting. It's awful. It's terrifying and you feel like puking and you are desperate for it to end. You can't put real danger aside when things get too scary and wait to read that part in daylight.

And if you have a crippling fear of calling for help, that awfulness is multiplied by a factor of a lot.

But as I sat at the table, letting the seconds go by, I realized something important. Caroline had asked for my help with her book, and I'd been happy to give it to her. And Javier and Marta had helped. And the seniors had helped—and really enjoyed it. People asked for help all the time, and people gave it all the time.

Gladly. Just because two police officers had scared me once—and they probably hadn't meant to scare me at all—didn't mean that asking for help was wrong.

Then I looked at it another way. Rosa needed *my* help. Rosa needed my help, and I needed help to help her. I was Vern the Pigeon, and Rosa was Gerald, and her broken hip was the battle, and I needed to contact the Absolute Authority....

I picked up the phone and shakily punched in 911.

107

A LADY ANSWERED MY 911 CALL. I was almost positive it was not the lady who had answered my previous one. They must have had more than one person answering, right?

"Great-Aunt Rosa fell down the stairs," I blurted at her. "She says she broke her hip. She's a nurse, so it probably isn't just a sprain. I'm not sure if this is an emergency, but she needs help."

"It sounds like an emergency to me," the lady said. "So we're going to send an ambulance, okay?" I nodded even though she couldn't see me. She asked me where we were, and I had to run outside the front door to get the house number. I was completely out of breath when I gave it to her.

"Calm down, hon," she told me. "The ambulance is on the way. Here's the thing, though. The storm brought some trees and wires down, so it may take longer than it usually would. I'm going to need your help, okay?"

So now the person I had called for help needed my help to help Rosa. You see how this works? It gets very tangled up.

"Okay," I said.

"I'm going to stay on the phone with you until the EMTs get there," she said. "You do what I tell you and your aunt will be fine."

She asked me a bunch of questions and told me a bunch of things to do and not to do. I went back down to the basement with some of the sheets from the furniture to put over Rosa, since there wasn't anything else around to keep her warm.

"Are they coming?" Alvin asked me. "Her eyes keep closing."

I nodded and pointed to the phone.

"We need to try to keep her awake," the lady said. "Can you talk to her? Take her mind off the pain?"

"We need to talk to her," I told Alvin. "Distract her."

"Aunt Rosa?" said Alvin, gently wiggling the hand he was still holding. "Can you hear me?"

It took a while for her to answer. "Yes," she said. "I hear you."

"You said you came down here for a book," said Alvin. "Do you like to read?"

"I love to read," said Rosa softly. "Vera Weintraub used to lend me . . . Rob's books. I have one . . . here." Her free hand scrabbled around on the floor beside her, and sure enough, there was a fat paperback there.

Rob's books! I thought. That's what she'd been doing. Borrowing a book from one of the boxes.

"It's too dark down here to read," said Alvin. "But my aunt wrote a book. Do you want me to tell you about it? It's very interesting."

"Sounds . . . good," said Rosa.

So Alvin started telling the story of *Gerald in the Warlock's Weir*, right from the beginning. And Rosa and I and the 911 operator listened until the ambulance arrived.

108

THE EMTS WERE TWO YOUNG WOMEN, and they were all business. They were used to giving orders and having people obey them. Then they met Great-Aunt Rosa.

I had gone upstairs to show them the way to the basement. They told me to stay in the kitchen, which I obediently did. When they arrived downstairs, I could hear them trying to get Alvin out of the way as well. I couldn't hear what Rosa said, only the responses from her rescuers. The conversation went something like this:

"The boy needs to wait upstairs while we—"

. . .

"Yes, ma'am."

"I'm sorry, ma'am, but you need to let go of the boy's hand so we can—"

. . .

"Yes, ma'am."

"Ma'am, you at least need to let go of his hand long enough for us to get you—"

. . .

"Yes, ma'am."

"How about if he—"

...

"Yes, ma'am."

The EMTs must have reached an agreement with Rosa, because Alvin arrived in the kitchen shortly after that. He was carrying Rosa's book and the sheets we had used to cover her. He dumped the sheets on the table but kept the book, I noticed.

"Are we going to get in trouble?" he asked me.

"No," I said. "This is a real emergency."

"I mean because we're trespassing," said Alvin. "Aren't all three of us trespassing here?"

I hadn't even thought about that, which was probably a good thing. "It doesn't matter," I told him as confidently as I could. "They're EMTs, not police."

"But don't they all know each other?"

I had no idea.

I did know that Alvin and I were damp, filthy, and reeked like storm drain and dog pee. We certainly didn't look or smell like two fine young lads who'd heard the cries of a lady in distress and heroically gone into a strange house to rescue her. But that was going to be our story. I outlined it for Alvin, and he readily agreed.

"Ma'am, it's possible you have other injuries," we heard from downstairs. "If we could just—"

...

"Yes, ma'am."

They brought Great-Aunt Rosa upstairs, and she reached for Alvin's hand immediately. Then the four of them headed out to the waiting ambulance.

"Ma'am, we can't have the boy in the ambulance. Is there a neighbor—"

. . .

"Yes, ma'am."

109

ALVIN AND I RODE IN THE back of the ambulance with Rosa to the hospital. Which was cool, but not as cool as it would have been if the siren had been blaring and we'd been whipping around corners and speeding through red lights. The ambulance went slowly because of all the branches lying in the streets from the storm. And also because Rosa was "stabilized," which meant we weren't in a big rush.

As soon as she was done batting away questions from the EMT riding in the back with us, Rosa asked Alvin to continue telling the story of Gerald. Which he did. He had a phenomenal memory, my little brother. He didn't leave out a single important detail as far as I could tell, and sometimes he used whole chunks of Caroline's words.

It was only then that I remembered the 911 operator. "Hello?" I said into my phone. "Are you still there?"

"I sure am, hon. You did great. Your aunt should be very proud of you."

"Thanks," I said. "And thank you for your help. I guess we can hang up now. You must have other emergencies you need to get to."

"As a matter of fact, I don't at the moment," she said. "I'm on break. Do you mind if I hang on a while? I want to hear how Gerald makes it past those pigeons."

I already knew Gerald's story, so as Alvin talked and Rosa and the 911 lady and the EMT listened, my mind was free to roam.

It didn't roam far. It roamed over to Great-Aunt Rosa. And her presence in the Old Weintraub Place. In the Old Weintraub basement. Borrowing Rob's books.

A bunch of facts started to crowd into my head, jostling for attention. Rosa had said she'd come over to the Old Weintraub Place to get away from Great-Aunt Marina. Javier had said Rosa went to the senior center to get away from Marina, but we never saw her there. Rosa liked to read Rob's books. Rosa often enjoyed a cup of coffee when she was reading. Rosa had been at Javier's when I fell off the trellis and Javier and Marta said the things to me that the ghost later quoted for Snarko and the Daredevil.

The ghost. Great-Aunt Rosa was the ghost.

It all made sense when I thought about it. Rosa had borrowed Rob's books when she and Mrs. Weintraub were neighbors, and she'd kept borrowing them after Mrs. Weintraub moved away. Maybe she had a key to the house. Then, when Marina moved in, instead of reading on the front porch, she'd moved into the Weintraub kitchen for some privacy. She'd been reading all those fantasies, so she was the perfect person to help with Caroline's book. She was the one who'd made it into a fantasy to begin with.

I looked over at Rosa, lying on the gurney, listening to Alvin tell her a story she already knew. A story she'd helped write. I reached into my pocket and felt the note I'd found on the kitchen table. Rosa had come up with a solution to Grampa's sacrifice, and it was in my pocket.

But it could wait.

110

WHEN THE AMBULANCE PULLED UP AT the hospital's emergency entrance, the EMT who was riding in the back turned to us and said, "Looks like we're going to have to rush her right into surgery."

"Why?" said Alvin. He clutched even harder at Rosa's hand.

Rosa didn't look nearly as alarmed as he did.

"To separate your hand from hers," said the EMT. Totally deadpan. No hint of a smile.

"You can let go now," Rosa told Alvin. "But don't forget you are a hero. No matter how filthy you are."

Alvin let go of Rosa. But before he moved away, I saw him slip Rob's book onto the gurney next to her. Her hand found it, and she smiled.

The EMTs rolled Rosa down a hall, and Alvin and I followed them.

They told us to sit in the waiting area, and they disappeared through a set of doors with Rosa.

After a while the EMTs emerged and walked over to us.

"She's going to be fine," one of them said. "But it's a good thing you called. You did the right thing, both of you."

"Nadia!" someone bellowed from across the room. "Simone! Is that you? Good to see you!"

The EMTs looked up at the familiar voice. Familiar to them, and familiar to me too. Marta was charging toward us, practically knocking various sick and injured people out of her way. Her left arm was in a cast and a sling, but she was waving it around excitedly.

"How's business?" Marta asked the EMTs when she got over to us.

"Not bad," one of them said. "We haven't seen you in a while. Nice bangs."

"Thanks," said Marta. "At first I didn't like them, but then they grew on me. *Grew* on me. Get it?"

The EMTs stared.

"I've been trimming them myself," Marta went on. "My mom can't confiscate *all* the scissors in the house."

The EMTs, who were trained to charge toward danger, each took a careful step away from Marta.

Then Marta noticed me and Alvin. "Alex!" she said. "Hey, Alvin! What are you guys doing here? And why are you so dirty? Did you get caught in a mud slide?"

"No, a storm sewer," said Alvin proudly.

"Like Gerald?" Marta asked.

"Yes!" said Alvin. "Only, he wouldn't fit. Not without liquid soap, anyway. I definitely determined that, didn't I, Alex?"

I nodded. "What happened to your arm?" I asked Marta.

"Broke it in two places!" she said.

"At circus camp?"

"Dud camp is more like it. 'Ooh, Marta, why aren't you using your safety harness?' 'Ooh, Marta, stop running away from your spotters!' They didn't let us take any risks at all."

"But you still managed to break your arm," an EMT pointed out.

"Right?" said Marta. "But it took almost a week."

"We gotta go," an EMT said.

"Yup. Be right there," the other told her.

The one who'd been driving left. The one who'd been in the back of the ambulance with us scuffed the toe of her shoe against the floor for a second before looking at Alvin and asking, "So, what was the name of that book you were describing? I need to find out how the battle ends."

111

MARTA SAT WITH ALVIN AND ME while her mom talked with the doctor. Her mom kept shaking her head, and the doctor kept shrugging.

"What was it like inside the storm drain?" Marta asked Alvin.

"Only my legs went inside," said Alvin. "It was kind of warm and—"

We never found out what else Alvin's legs thought of being inside the storm drain, because we heard our names called across the room. By Dad.

Oops. Dad. I'd forgotten that he would have gotten home by now and would be wondering why the two of us weren't there. How had he found us here? He didn't look angry, though, as he came over. He looked excited and was grinning hugely.

"Oh good, you're here," he said. "Mom and I must have gotten our signals crossed. She said you'd be at home, but when you weren't, I figured she brought you with her. *What* have you two been doing? Never mind. Any news on Lu yet?"

Oops. Mom and Lulu. I'd forgotten about Lu's accident. They were here at the hospital too.

"Um, no," I said to Dad. "Not yet. They're probably stitching up her foot."

"Her foot?" said Dad.

"Maybe," I said. "She broke her water, so I guess she stepped on some glass. It's taking a while, so maybe she severed a toe and they're reattaching it."

Marta was listening avidly and nodding. "They could have brought the toe stub in a plastic bag," she said.

"But maybe she broke her toe," I went on, "and they're putting a tiny cast on it. That would take some time, wouldn't it?"

"A cast that small would definitely require extra time," Marta agreed.

My dad was chuckling, and so was Alvin, which was annoying.

"Her water broke," said Dad. "It means the baby's on the way."

Alvin gave me a duh look, but Marta was as confused as I was. "How would having a baby make you drop water on your foot?" she asked.

I'll spare you the ultra-embarrassing discussion that followed, during which Marta asked way too many questions and Dad answered them in way too much detail.

Eventually, I decided to go to the men's room to get away from it. Also to wash some of the grime off. Also to pee. It had been a long afternoon.

112

I WAS TRYING TO WASH MY hair in the men's-room sink using the foaming hand soap from the pump dispenser when the door opened and someone immediately started laughing. Hard.

I looked up, water and soap streaming into my eyes, and saw Javier, his hands on his knees, literally bent over with laughter.

"Oh, I wish I had my camera," he said much, much later, when he'd gotten ahold of himself.

What was this, a class reunion at the hospital? Who was going to turn up next? Our teachers?

"What are you doing here?" I asked Javier.

"We got a call that Great-Aunt Rosa had fallen."

"But weren't you at the beach? How did you get here so fast?"

"My dad drove like a maniac. I think the minivan caught air a couple times." He eyed me. "What are you doing bathing in the hospital men's room?"

I dried myself off with paper towels as best I could while I explained about Alvin and the storm drain and the thunderstorm and the nonrescue dog and the Old Weintraub Place and Rosa.

"She's going to be fine," I told him when I got to the end.

"That's good," he said. "She's tough. That's what Dad kept saying on the way here."

"She is tough. I know that for a fact. I know another fact about her too."

"Oh, yeah?"

"Great-Aunt Rosa is the ghostwriter."

"She *is*? Great-Aunt *Rosa*? No *way*!"

Javier is a talented filmmaker but a terrible actor. He should definitely stay behind the camera.

"You already knew," I said.

"*What?* No! This comes as a total surprise to me. A complete shock—"

I threw a balled-up paper towel at his head. He ducked.

"Fine," he said. "She's called me an imp since I was two. As soon as I heard that name . . ."

"Why didn't you tell us?"

"I didn't want to ruin your fun."

"Fun? I've been sleeping with a night-light!"

"Humpty Dumpty?"

"It doesn't matter."

"Okay, I guess I didn't want to ruin *my* fun," Javier confessed. "Or Marta's."

"We're not telling Marta, are we?"

"No way."

113

ALVIN, DAD, AND I WERE EATING with Mom in the hospital cafeteria when Caroline found us.

Mom had joined us in the waiting room as soon as Caroline arrived and took over the official "birthing partner" duties. Mom had taken one look at Alvin and me and marched us to the men's room to clean up (in my case, again). When she asked how we'd gotten so filthy, Alvin told her he'd slipped and landed in a mud puddle and I'd fallen in when I tried to help him. He claimed his sneakers had been lost during the struggle. The string of lies spooled out so easily, it was almost disturbing to witness.

Fortunately, both parents were so excited about the baby that they didn't ask too many follow-up questions. In fact, I think they both still assume that the other brought us to the hospital that day. Alvin and I have certainly never set them straight.

Caroline's cheeks were pink and her eyes were dangerously shiny as she rushed across the cafeteria to our table.

"She's here!" she told us. "She's here and she's great and so is Lu. Come and see!"

We finished up as quickly as we could without choking, then

rushed to the maternity ward to meet the newest member of the family.

Lulu was sitting up in bed holding the baby when we got to her room. Caroline hovered around them like a crazed bird around a nest. The baby, wrapped like a burrito in a blanket, was asleep.

When we'd all oohed and aahed for a while, Lulu motioned Alvin over to the side of the bed. She held the sleeping baby up like a gift and said, "I believe this belongs to you."

Alvin's gigantic vocabulary failed him. He just gaped at the baby. "Huh?"

"She's yours," said Lulu. "Don't you remember? I wanted to change the TV channel that time, and you made me promise you my firstborn. So here she is! Never let it be said that I don't keep my promises."

Alvin held up his hands like he was surrendering. Or maybe he didn't want to get baby on them. "That's okay," he said.

"What?" Lulu said. "You don't want her? Are you sure?"

"I'm sure," said Alvin. "When I made you promise that, I had no idea what I was getting into."

Lulu laughed as Caroline swooped in and took the baby from her. "You and me both, kiddo," she said.

114

"WE'RE CALLING HER ALANA," CAROLINE TOLD us the next day when we went back to the hospital to visit.

"That's lovely," said Mom. "We're going to run out of names that begin with Al if you have more kids."

Lu, who had appeared to be asleep, barked a laugh at that without opening her eyes.

"Let's not rush into more kids until we see how this first one goes," said Caroline.

I thought about how much easier Alana's life would be without a younger sibling to mess with her stuff and require yanking out of storm drains. Then again, if Alvin hadn't gotten himself stuck, what would have happened to Aunt Rosa? And who would I blame for the dirty dishes in the sink if I didn't have a little brother?

I knew it was up to Caroline and Lulu to decide about another kid, but a shortage of Al names shouldn't stop them.

"You could call the next one Albert," I said.

I had something important to share with Caroline, though it was smeared and wrinkled from its time in my damp pocket yesterday.

I guided her out into the hallway as Mom, Dad, and Grandma Sally took turns sniffing Alana's head and Alvin explored the room's medical equipment.

"I think I have the solution to the problem of Grampa's sacrifice," I said to Caroline.

"Really? I was in tears writing that scene. Actual tears. Can you believe it?"

I could. She'd no doubt gone through a lot of linty tissues that day. "I think he can make a sacrifice without dying," I said. "It's written down here." I pulled the paper out of my pocket.

"That looks like a rag," said Caroline.

"It's a rag now, but it used to be a piece of paper."

"I'll have to take your word for that."

"Anyway, I can tell you what it says. But we also need to go somewhere. In the hospital. There's someone you have to meet."

115

I HAD ARRIVED AT THE HOSPITAL before the rest of my family that morning. I'd gotten a ride with Javier when he and his parents went to see Rosa. I needed to talk to Rosa before I talked to Caroline.

While Javier's parents were getting coffee downstairs, I saw my chance. But before I could open my mouth, Rosa started talking. Speaking quickly and quietly, like the three of us were spies meeting in an alley, she said that she'd told Javier's parents she'd fallen at home and called the ambulance herself. Rosa said she would be glad to tell *my* parents about Alvin's and my heroics, but—

I stopped her right there. "Alvin and I were trespassing," I said. "We'd both rather you didn't mention it to our parents."

"You weren't trespassing," said Rosa. "You're quite welcome anytime. It's my property. I bought it this past winter."

"You did?" said Javier.

"I was thinking I'd rent it out," said Rosa. "But meanwhile it's a good place to be alone once in a while. Marina can drive me nuts."

When Javier and I had digested that chunk of information,

I got around to what I'd wanted to ask Rosa. Which was if it was okay to tell Caroline about her contributions to the book.

"When did you figure out it was me?" Rosa asked. "I thought I was covering my tracks pretty well."

"Oh," I hedged. "You know, a while ag—"

"Yesterday," Javier interrupted.

Not surprisingly, Rosa said no, that she wanted her ghost-writing to stay a secret. "I was perfectly happy to let you think I was a ghost," said Rosa. "And I would prefer to remain anonymous."

"But my aunt thinks I came up with those ideas," I said. "She thinks I'm some kind of genius. I can't live with that now that I know they were yours."

"He can't live a lie," Javier said solemnly.

"I see," said Rosa. "All right. Why don't you bring her by and we can discuss it."

As I led Caroline to Rosa's room, I read her the note/rag about Grampa's sacrifice.

"'When Grampa and Gerald are sent to their world by the warlock, Grampa has been badly weakened by his time in the vortex. He doesn't have the magical strength to make a new slip-stream big enough for both of them, only for Gerald. He gives all his remaining magic so Gerald can go back. But Grampa can't go with him. Grampa can never go back to the magical world.'

"So Grampa's still alive," I said. "And Gerald can see him when he goes home. But he makes a huge sacrifice, and Gerald has to take it from there in the alternate world. Plus, there's no way Grampa could fit into a storm drain. Even Gerald is going to have a hard time with that. He might need something slippery—"

"A potion!" said Caroline. "He can use a potion for that. This is perfect, Alex. You are such a genius!" She grabbed me in the hospital corridor and hugged me and kissed my forehead, and I think a some doctors saw the whole thing.

"Actually," I said, "I'm not in any way a genius. I didn't come up with that solution. And there are a bunch of other ideas in the book that I also didn't come up with. I want you to meet the person who did."

116

BY THE TIME WE GOT TO Rosa's room, I had told Caroline what ideas Rosa had contributed without going into the whole ghost thing. I gave her the impression that Rosa had just joined my discussions with Javier about the book when we were at his house.

Maybe it was the thrill of Alana's arrival that kept Caroline from giving me another lecture about sharing the book without her permission. Or maybe she'd given up on that after the Battle of the Senior Center. Either way, she didn't get into it with me.

Caroline practically knelt in front of Rosa when we got to her bedside, thanking her and telling her how amazing she was. Rosa and I were both embarrassed. Javier was amused. Rosa kept waving her hand at Caroline like she was swatting away a gnat.

But Caroline-the-gnat was persistent. Most gnats are, in my experience. "I can't thank you enough," she said to Rosa. "You turned the whole book around. More than once. And your idea for Grampa's sacrifice? It makes complete emotional sense. I'm so grateful for your help."

Then she started talking about giving Rosa credit in the book itself, and that was when Rosa told Javier and me to go wait outside.

We went into the hallway and closed the door. We could still hear Caroline, whose voice was higher pitched, but not Rosa. It was easy to figure out who won that discussion, though. It went like this:

"I'm sure we can work out some way to give you—"

. . .

"Oh, but I very much want to—"

. . .

"But you deserve to be—"

. . .

"I understand, but—"

. . .

"Yes, ma'am."

. . .

"Yes, ma'am."

Caroline was pale when she emerged from Rosa's room, and her hair was sticking out all over her head like a mad scientist's.

"I think I may have promised her my next child if I ever reveal her part in this book to anyone," she said, trying to gather her puffs of hair into a ponytail and failing. "I don't think I'm allowed even to say her name in public."

"She's tough," said Javier.

"No kidding," said Caroline. "I definitely did promise her Alvin, by the way. She wants him to come read to her. Apparently, she finds his voice soothing."

117

SO THAT'S THE TRUE STORY OF R. R. Knight, the mysterious author of the Gerald books.

R. R. Knight isn't just a pen name for my aunt Caroline. Or for my aunt Caroline and me. It's a name that includes Caroline (mostly), me (for danger, trial stunts, epic battle—you're welcome—sensory details, and boringness patrol), Great-Aunt Rosa (for major, major plot ideas and making it a fantasy), Javier (for filming and magical-plants idea and Snarko personality), Marta (for ghost pestering and stunts and Daredevil personality), Nate (for Grampa sayings and battle strategy), Ellen (for gory details), Alvin (for battle-film participants and storm-drain stunt), Henry (for moon head), the librarian in the children's room (for book suggestions and Book 2's Lost Librarian personality), and a bunch of authors of fantasies for kids and adults from the library and from Rob Weintraub's book collection.

As for the name, Caroline says she picked "Knight" because it's in the middle of the alphabet, which puts the books in the middle of the shelf at the bookstore and the middle of the stacks at the library. She insists that "R. R." does stand for something, but she won't tell me what it is.

I think I know, though. I think it stands for "reluctant reader." Which I still am, I guess, although I'm a voracious listener. You have to find the right books, as Ellen said, but you also have to find the right delivery system. Mine is through the ears, not the eyes. And usually while I'm running—I can't get restless if I'm moving.

I still run everywhere, although I don't feel like I have to anymore. My brush with real danger put my worries about potential danger to rest, I guess. Now I run because I enjoy it. I even joined the cross-country team at school.

And how do I feel about calling 911? I haven't had to do it since Great-Aunt Rosa broke her hip. But I feel like I could if I had to. Maybe doing it again took care of that fear. But I think it had more to do with finally telling someone what happened the first time.

It came out by accident. I brought Rosa some audiobooks in the hospital, and when I apologized for hesitating before I called 911 for her, I ended up describing my encounter with the police. I said that, looking back, the officers probably hadn't meant to scare me. "Maybe I blew that up in my head," I said.

"That's possible," she said. "You have a big imagination."

"Are you kidding? I have no imagination," I said. "Ask Javier."

I'd never seen Aunt Rosa laugh before, but when she did, she reminded me of Javier. She almost fell out of bed. "Everyone has an imagination," she said when she'd gotten ahold of herself.

I still do Caroline's stunts, along with Marta, of course. (Alvin retired from stunts after the storm drain and is in charge of potions now—he prefers indoor work.) Marta, Javier, and I recently signed up for a daylong white-water-rafting course to help with Book 3's Spewing Spume scene. Javier is looking forward to trying out his new waterproof camera.

I still haven't gotten around to confessing to Caroline that my "imaginative details" for her books are based on actual stunts. I had planned to tell her after the end of Book 1, but then Book 2 came along, and now 3, and . . . I'll tell her when she's done with the whole series. Definitely then.

"But wait a minute," you're probably thinking. "Didn't you say at the very beginning that you would rather dive into the back of a garbage truck with your mouth open than be famous? Why write a book like this if that's true? Won't this book make you famous as Gerald's stunt double?"

My response to those excellent questions has two parts. First, there's no way this book is going to make me famous. It's not exactly R. R. Knight–level excitement, is it?

And second, my name's not really Alex Harmon.

ACKNOWLEDGMENTS

THIS IS A BOOK ABOUT GETTING help writing a book, which makes the acknowledgments seem especially important. I'll start at the beginning and hope for the best.

First thanks go to Karen and her voracious-reader niece, who generously (and inadvertently) gave me the idea for this book. And to Debbie, who had the faith to invite me, writing unseen, to her critique group.

Mere words can't express my gratitude to the critique group, for being so welcoming and supportive, for laughing in the right places and pointing out the boring parts, and for introducing me to SCBWI. Many thanks to SCBWI New England, for all they do for aspiring writers and for introducing me to my agent. To my agent, Joan Paquette, for her quirky sense of humor and unflagging optimism and for introducing me to my editor. To my editor, Karen Wojtyla, for her aunt-appreciation and her expert wielding of the Red Pen of Inspiration.

A vortex of thanks to the rest of the gang at McElderry Books and Simon & Schuster: Nicole Fiorica, for her great ideas and expert guidance throughout the process; copyeditor Lynn

Kavanaugh, for the oh-so-careful read and gentle reminders that hair grows; proofreader Mandy Veloso; managing editor Bridget Madsen; production manager Elizabeth Blake-Linn; designer Rebecca Syracuse; and publicist Chantal Gersch. Thanks as well to the amazing Linzie Hunter, for the perfect cover art and for putting my name in a zucchini.

A huge thank-you to my colleagues past and present, including but not limited to Ben, Debbie (again), Jayne, Karen (again), Linda, Mary, Mike, Pamela, Peg, and Peggy, for their friendship and gross stories and for discreetly not mentioning any errors they may spot herein.

Special thanks to Mom, Auntie Karen, Jon, Jennifer, Christina, Diana, Suze, Jay, Carter, and all the Fawcetts and Williamsons, for laughing with me and also sometimes at me, and for not acting too shocked about this whole turn of events. To Lisa, for obsessing about the same books I did and do; and to Mike, Ted, and Marshall, for off-beat clapping.

Finally and especially, unending thanks to Clara and Stephen, for filling my house with books and my heart with love.

TURN THE PAGE FOR A SNEAK PEEK AT

WELCOME TO DWEEB CLUB

Betsy Uhrig

THE ORIGINS OF THE FLOUNDER BAY UPPER SCHOOL
H.A.I.R. Club are shrouded in mystery. Or maybe cloaked
in mystery. Or at least wearing a heavy cardigan of mystery. As the official club historian, I tried to figure it out,
and you can decide whether I was at all successful. I do
know one thing, though: None of us would have joined if
Glamorous Steve hadn't gotten there first. And if we hadn't
joined, our lives would have turned out very differently.
I'm not just saying this for dramatic effect—it is a fact.

But let's start at the beginning. A history should go in
order, after all.

It was the second week of seventh grade. I was still finding my way around the building, which was way bigger
and more crowded than elementary school, and mentally

labeling kids I didn't know (Vegan Lunch, Stork Legs, British Accent, et cetera). When I walked into school that morning, there were folding tables lining both sides of the main hall. The tables had posters hanging in front of them advertising various school clubs. Two or three upbeat kids who looked way too cheerful for that time of day sat behind each table.

All these upbeat kids were trying to get other, lower-beat kids to join their clubs, offering enticements like mini-muffins, and those rubber bracelets that really hurt if you shot them at people, and even tiny Frisbees with FBUS ULTIMATE FRISDEE (oops) printed on them.

It was my intention to walk right by these tables and keep going until I got to my locker. It was not my inten-tion to sign up for a club that morning. I like to take my time making big decisions, and joining a school club was a big decision. Your choice of clubs could determine a whole new set of friends and also what kinds of labels would get slapped on *you*. It was way too early—in the day and the year—for me to be making a decision with these kinds of life-changing consequences.

But I didn't make it to my locker. My friend Glamor-ous Steve was standing at the last table in the row, and he grabbed the strap of my backpack as I was hurrying past, causing me to lurch to a stop.

"Jason," he said. "Wait up."

"What?"

"I'm going to sign up for"—he looked down at the sheet

of paper that was the only thing on the table—"H.A.I.R. Club. You should too."

No one, upbeat or not, was sitting behind the table. There were no posters. There was no swag. There was a sign-up sheet with a coffee ring on it and *New This Year! See Ms. Grossman, Faculty Adviser, for Details!* scrawled across the bottom in red pen. Ms. Grossman was my US History teacher, and even this early in the year, I was all too familiar with her red scrawls.

"Is this a joke?" I said. I glanced at the sheet with its un-filled-in blanks. There wasn't even a crummy pencil next to it. "There's no one signed up at all. And what is Hair Club, anyway?"

"It's not Hair Club," said Steve. "It's H.A.I.R. Club. It's initials."

"So what do the initials stand for?"

"No idea. Maybe 'Hair And Its Relatives'?"

I could see why that might interest Steve. He had perfect hair and he put real effort into its upkeep. It did not, however, interest me and my normal-to-greasy, effort-free hair.

"So it *is* Hair Club," I said. "And what's a hair relative? Fingernails? Sorry. Not interested."

I had turned to head for my locker when Steve put a hand on my shoulder.

"Here's the thing," he said. "Whatever it stands for—and it might have nothing to do with hair—H.A.I.R. Club is brand-new. No one is signed up yet. We'd be the first members."

I shrugged his hand off my shoulder. But I turned back to face him. "So?"

"So if we join now, as seventh graders, we'll be club officers by the time we're in, like, eighth grade."

Now he had my attention.

"If we're the first to sign up," I said, thinking out loud, "wouldn't we be club officers right away? It's only fair."

Steve was nodding at my brilliant logic. Or maybe at my willingness to go along with him. He handed me a pen. "We'd be in charge of a brand-new club. In seventh grade. Think about it," he said.

I was already signing my name.

A word about Glamorous Steve before we go on. Steve's family had moved to Flounder Bay the summer before sixth grade. There are three kinds of new kids, as I'm sure you know. There's the weird new kid, the bland new kid, and the glamorous new kid.

Steve, who was from California and had that perfect hair and a smile that pretty much made a cartoon twinkly *ping* whenever he flashed it, was as glamorous as it got in Flounder Bay. His glamour was upped by the fact that a hopelessly bland kid also named Steve had moved to town at the same time. So there was Steve and there was Glamorous Steve. And then, for most of us, there was just Glamorous Steve, the other kid having been forgotten. Or maybe he changed his name. Doesn't matter. He won't appear in this history again.

Glamorous Steve had a talent for doing even the geeki-
est things with such infectious enthusiasm that he made
them not just acceptable but downright trendy. He was a
long-distance runner. Boring, you say? Yes, indeed. Unless
Glamorous Steve was moving effortlessly past you, his
glorious hair streaming behind him. He collected stamps.
Game over, you're thinking. And ordinarily you'd be right.
But he made it work. Somehow, he made it work.

So I knew I was safe signing up for anything Steve was
a part of. In fact, even as Steve was writing his name below
mine on the H.A.I.R. Club sign-up sheet, his glamour was
rippling through the hallway and other kids were falling
into line behind him. They didn't care what he was signing
up for—if Glamorous Steve was in, they wanted in too.

I should add that fully half of them balked when they
got to the point of actually writing their names. After all,
they had no idea what H.A.I.R. stood for. And they could
see for themselves the empty table and its pathetic sign-
up sheet. Even Steve's glamour wasn't enough for them
to risk their reputations on what looked like the losingest
club ever. I don't blame them. And I'm glad only ten kids
signed up.

Those others will never know what they missed.

THE FIRST-EVER MEETING OF THE FLOUNDER BAY
Upper School H.A.I.R. Club took place on September 9, a
Tuesday, at three o'clock in the afternoon. Eleven people
were present, and I'm going to describe each of them
briefly, since almost all of them have a major part in this
history.

First, there was Ms. Grossman: history teacher and
club adviser. She had a big vocabulary and a mean red pen
and wasn't afraid to use either.

Next, Jason Sloan: me—your narrator. I hate those scenes
in books where the poor narrator tries to describe what they
see in a mirror and point out their flaws to seem humble. I
was extremely ordinary, kind of scrawny, often mistaken for
a sixth grader when I was in seventh. Will that do?

"Glamorous" Steve Hendricks: who has already been introduced. I don't think he needs any more description.

Nikhil Singh: a friend of Steve's from cross-country. I sat behind Nikhil in history, so I was familiar with the unusual angle at which his ears attached to his head. I also knew that he was easily irritated, based on his grouching about my "tuneless humming" during quizzes.

Harriet "Hoppy" Hopkins: daughter of the owners of Hopkins Hairnets, the second-biggest company in Flounder Bay. Hoppy was noticeable around school for her ultra-curly hair, which would have driven her hairnet-manufacturing ancestors up a wall, and her, um, commanding voice.

Andrew Vernicky: the tall redheaded boy from my science class whose laid-back attitude almost covered up how smart he was. He never raised his hand, but when he was called on, he was always right. He once corrected the teacher.

Sonia Patel: possibly the most agreeable person I'd ever encountered. Even her outfits were agreeable. She managed to color-coordinate her backpack and shoes with her clothes every day. Sonia had huge brown eyes and always wore a (matching) hairband in her dark brown hair.

Laura Andersen: the shy blond girl from my math class. I swear I'd met clams that were more outgoing than Laura was.

Vincent Chen: How do you describe your best friend since kindergarten? Vincent had messy black hair and a goofy smile. Good enough? He had joined all the school's clubs on a dare from his older sister. Vincent never could resist a dare, something I myself occasionally took advantage of.

Two other kids whose names I never found out. Their descriptions aren't important, for reasons I'll get to later.

The interesting thing to note here is that all the club members were seventh graders. Coincidence? Not really.

At Flounder Bay Upper School, seventh through twelfth grades are in one building together because the town is too small to need separate ones. This meant that any kid who was older than seventh grade already knew about the school's clubs and wouldn't have bothered with that lone H.A.I.R. table at the end of the row. They knew what clubs they wanted to join, and they joined them.

In fact, Vincent could have gotten away with not signing up for H.A.I.R. Club, because his sister had no idea it existed. But Vincent has a strong code of honor. Plus, I made him.

Anyway, back to the first meeting . . .

Ms. Grossman started things off.

"Welcome to H.A.I.R. Club," she said, trying to sound enthusiastic in the face of this small and skeptical-looking group. "This is the first year that Flounder Bay Upper School has offered H.A.I.R. Club, and I'm so glad you've decided to join!" You could hear her tossing in that exclamation point with effort. "I'm Ms. Grossman, as those of you who are my US History students know. And I am your club adviser. Which is awkward, because I have to admit that I have no idea what H.A.I.R. stands for.

"Here's the backstory," Ms. Grossman went on, taking a seat on the edge of the desk at the front of the room. "This past summer, a very successful entrepreneur who wishes to remain anonymous offered the services of his company to install a state-of-the-art security system here. He very generously donated this to the school with one stipulation."

Ms. Grossman, I knew from being in her class, constantly used words like "entrepreneur" and "stipulation" without defining them. When someone asked what one of her words meant, she'd tell them to "write it down and look it up—you'll learn it better that way." I tended not to bother, which might explain the number of red corrections on my papers.

"That stipulation," Ms. Grossman continued, "was that we start a club here at school called H.A.I.R. Club, and that its members take charge of the security system."

Now we were all sort of eyeing one another.

"Ha!" barked Ms. Grossman. "I see some questions on your faces. And maybe the first one is, who in their right mind would put a student club in charge of a brand-new state-of-the-art security system? The same thing occurred to me. But the donor was quite clear about it. Club members *only* will monitor the system." She raised a finger and added, "Which might be a good thing, because I don't think any of the adults here could even begin to figure it out."

One of the nameless kids raised his hand.

"Yes?" said Ms. Grossman.

"So this club doesn't have anything to do with hair?" he asked.

"No, it doesn't," Ms. Grossman said. "H.A.I.R. must stand for something, but the donor never indicated what it was."

The kid who'd asked the question stood up, along with the girl next to him.

"We thought H.A.I.R. spelled *hair*," the girl said as they headed for the door.

"Well, it does, of course," said Ms. Grossman. "Although in this case—"

But they'd already opened the door. The girl practically dove into the hallway. The boy lingered long enough to look around and say quietly, "'Welcome to Dweeb Club' is more like it" before he made his escape. I think I was the only one who heard him, since I was nearest the door.

Okay, so this new club involved security cameras and computer equipment. But that didn't make it Dweeb Club just because some chucklehead said so. Did it? This wasn't a roomful of dweebs. We had Glamourous Steve and . . . and . . .

Uh-oh. What had I gotten myself into?

EXPERIENCE THE MAGIC AND MISCHIEF

OF THE BOGGART AND HIS FRIENDS IN THIS CLASSIC SERIES FROM NEWBERY MEDAL WINNER SUSAN COOPER

"As long as writers with Susan Cooper's skill continue to publish, magic is always available."
—*New York Times Book Review*

★"A lively story, compelling from first page to last."
—*School Library Journal*, starred review of *The Boggart*

★"An imaginative and compelling tale."
—*Publishers Weekly*, starred review of *The Boggart and the Monster*

"The Boggart remains as comical, fey, unpredictable, and thoroughly entertaining as ever."
—*Kirkus Reviews*, on *The Boggart Fights Back*

PRINT AND EBOOK EDITIONS AVAILABLE
From Margaret K. McElderry Books
simonandschuster.com/kids

NICK HAS A PLAN
to win the local batboy contest

STEP 1: Lie to his parents.

STEP 2: Blackmail his uncle.

STEP 3: Dodge the school bully.

STEP 4: Stay one step ahead of a
2000-pound rhinoceros.

What could possibly go wrong?

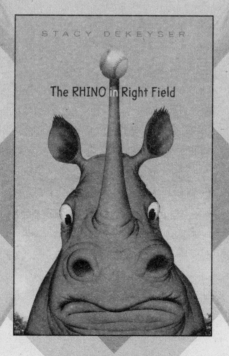

STACY DEKEYSER

The RHINO in Right Field

★ "A winner in every way."—*Kirkus Reviews*, starred review

PRINT AND EBOOK EDITIONS AVAILABLE

From Margaret K. McElderry Books ◆ simonandschuster.com/kids